ENCHANTED EMPORIUM

I

Enchanted Emporium is published by Capstone Young Readers
A Capstone imprint
1710 Roe Crest Drive
North Mankato, Minnesota 56003
www.capstoneyoungreaders.com

First published in the United States in 2014 by Capstone

© 2012 Atlantyca Dreamfarm s.r.l., Italy
© 2014 for this book in English language (Capstone Young Readers)
Text by Pierdomenico Baccalario
Illustrations by Iacopo Bruno
Translated by Maria Allen
Original edition published by Edizioni Piemme S.p.A., Italy
Original title: Una valigia di stelle

Cataloging-in-Publication Data is available on the Library of Congress website.
ISBN: 978-1-4342-6516-6 (library binding)
ISBN: 978-1-4342-6519-7 (paperback)
ISBN: 978-1-62370-039-3 (paper-over-board)

Summary: Have you heard of Cinderella's glass slipper? What about Sinbad the Sailor's Flying Carpet? There are many magical items in the world — but only one place where they're safe: the Enchanted Emporium. For centuries, seven families have competed for ownership of the store — and some of them are willing to do whatever it takes to get their hands on the powerful objects housed within. Only Aiby Lily and her friend Finley have what it takes to stop the shop from falling into the wrong hands.

Designer: Alison Thiele

Printed in the United States of America in Stevens Point Wisconsin.
092013   007765WZS14

SUITCASE OF STARS

by Pierdomenico Baccalario · Illustrations by Iacopo Bruno

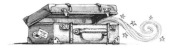

capstone
young readers

TABLE OF CONTENTS

Chapter
ONE

PATCHES,
DOUG,
& ME

My name is Finley McPhee. Finley sounds just like it looks: FINN-Lee. Anyway, I've had a pretty good life. I wasn't the smartest kid in school or a great rugby player like my brother, but I never argued much with my parents or fought with my friends. Not that I had many friends. I preferred to be alone whenever I could, away from bullies and drama.

I didn't get to see much of the world outside where I lived. I knew that the main road out of my village would eventually take you to Inverness or Edinburgh, two bigger cities that were full of people and — according to our teachers — great opportunities. Though they never did explain what kinds of opportunities they meant.

I grew up in the village of Applecross in the far northern part of Scotland. It was a nice enough place to grow up. It had everything you needed to survive, but not much in the way of distractions. Applecross had two roads, a main square with a small fountain that never worked, Mr. Fionnbhurd's pub, a supermarket, and various other stores.

The farms were located just south of the village. Nearly all of them were involved in raising sheep, just like my father's farm. North of the village was the mill where they used to make the wheat. Only old lady Cumai lived there now.

Higher up in the hills, on the heathland, were the remains of a large deserted castle. Cumai herself claimed the place was haunted on the thirteenth day of every month. On the opposite side was the cold and murky sea. On windy days, the sky was clear and the clouds sped by like wool through the threads of a loom. But when the wind dropped and the tide receded, clouds of mosquitoes would swarm the beach. But that didn't stop me and Patches from searching the beach for treasures.

Yes, treasures! You might not believe me, but Patches and I actually found a message in a bottle once. Patches was my dog. He was as tall as my knees and had long ears and shaggy fur. He found the bottle, actually. I put it in my bedroom along with the other pieces in my collection of rare finds, including chunks of metal, pieces of driftwood, and strange rocks. I labeled each of them with names like "Ligneous Steganosaurus Bone" or "Dry Leaves from the City of Doucumber." I'm not sure if a Steganosaurus ever really existed, or if there actually was a city named Doucumber. I just made up the names on the labels so that Doug, my brother, wouldn't try to steal them.

Doug was obsessed with rugby, girls, and being a total idiot. At the time, he was sixteen and had already dropped out of school. That was probably the only thing we had in common: I didn't care about finishing school, either.

Viper. That's what my brother nicknamed me. I think he chose it because I used to crouch down in the grass and hurl myself at him when we were little. Or maybe it was because I used to lie on the rocks in the sun all the time. I hated being called Viper, but there wasn't anything I could do about it. Once a nickname sticks, it stays with you forever.

Anyway, it was true: I did like sitting on the rocks — especially the ones along the curve of the Baelanch Ba. The name Baelanch Ba might sound fake like the names on my labels, but it's actually Gaelic for "Oxen Road." We

just called it the Coastal Road, and it ran along the entire coast. There were several huge stacks of rocks next to the road that were almost as big as the ancient dolmen, which are basically big tables made of boulders. I used to climb on top of them, sit with my legs crossed, and gaze out at the islands on the other side of the sea.

When I was young, my father taught me the islands' names in a particular order, saying it had always been done that way in Applecross. First came the islets to the north where the clouds seemed to come from. Then, slowly, you traced your finger along the islands until you got to Skyle, the largest one. It was black, eerie, and surrounded by shadows. My father promised me we would visit the island of Skyle on my fourteenth birthday, which was less than a year away. I was looking forward to it.

As I said, life was good. That is, until the Lily clan arrived and everything changed.

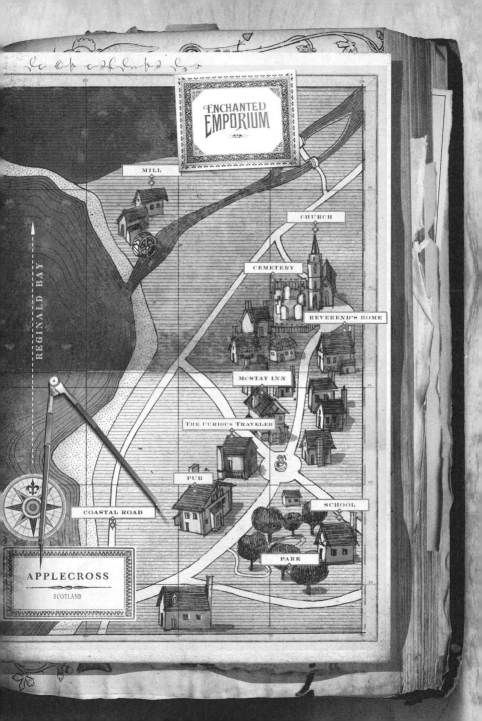

Chapter
TWO

THE WIDOW,
STINKY PUDDLES,
& BAD NEWS

The stream where I liked to fish didn't have a name. Old lady Cumai used to call it Calghorn Dinn, which means "stinky puddles" in the language of the Little People. That was a pretty good description of the spots where stagnant water formed and all kinds of things had fallen in and rotted. But once you knew it as well as I did, the Calghorn was actually a pretty awesome river.

To get there, you had to jump over the first few puddles and head north until you found an oak tree with a goat's skull hanging from it. Underneath the skull was a sign that read "NO TRESPASSING." Anyway, you ignored the sign and take the path on the left. Then you'd come to a small white beach with water so clear

that you can see fish swimming in it. Once you saw the place, you'd understand why I spent my free time there.

During the last week before the Lily family arrived and everything changed, the weather was perfect. Thankfully, school was closed for the summer. Well, to be honest, there were a few days of school left, but I'd decided that it was already over for me. I couldn't waste any more time sitting inside at a desk and memorizing my times tables or trying to remember what day Napoleon Bonaparte lost the Battle of Waterloo. I mean, does that stuff even do you any good? Not for me. And not for the fish I caught, either.

I hid my brother's fishing pole inside a tree that had been hollowed out by lightning. As for the tackle, I'd taught myself to make fishing flies all by myself — it's the only time I've actually found a book to be useful. As soon as I'd finished reading it, I returned it to the bookstore.

I made the flies while I waited for fish to bite. I had all the equipment with me: a hammer and a flat stone for curving wire into a hook, a pair of scissors to sharpen the hook, a few pieces of shiny aluminum, and some feathers I'd gotten from Mrs. Bigelov at the deli. I even colored the lures myself using dye that Meb McCameron, the dressmaker, had given me.

Nothing was biting that day, but fishing was never the main reason I went there. I just liked relaxing in the warm summer weather. Soft, white pollen hovered in the air beneath the blazing midday sun. If I'd stayed there until evening, I would have seen dragonflies gliding over the surface of the lake. But I couldn't stay much longer — my parents thought I was at school, so I had to return home shortly after the school bell rang.

I glanced at my watch. The face had an ivory dial, and the golden hands had sharp points like miniature spears. The numbers were all raised — except for number seven, which had fallen off. I'd always thought that it wasn't a coincidence, since seven was the hour I hated most of all: it was the time I had to wake up on school days.

It was almost time for school to get out. If I left now, I'd have just enough time to walk through the woods, slip by the flour mill without old lady Cumai seeing me, and then arrive in the village a few seconds before the bell rang.

"Come on, Patches!" I shouted. My dog looked up at me from under his ears. It looked like he was trying to move them with his eyebrows. "Let's go, goofball!"

I picked up the fishing rod and wound the line around it, making sure to place the hook in a lump of cork so that the line wouldn't get tangled. Then I carefully placed

everything back into the tree trunk, threw my school bag onto my shoulder, and headed back toward town.

It took me about fifteen minutes to reach the black-roofed buildings of Applecross. I entered the village in front of Mr. Everett's souvenir shop, The Curious Traveler, and crossed the square. I walked along the village wall, which was made up of stones that were fished out of the sea, and then snuck behind the school. Everything was going exactly according to plan.

When I heard the school bell ring, I was already on the other side of the building. I hadn't seen that side of that horrible school very often. Its crumbling walls and barred windows made it look like a prison. In fact, the only difference between the two was that you could get out of prison in less than five years on good behavior.

I took the road that led home to the farm, whistling as I walked. Soon I'd reached the dress shop.

"Hello, Ms. McCameron," I said.

Meb smiled at me. "Hey, Finn," she said.

"Thanks again for the dyes," I said.

"My pleasure," she said, and went back to work on a dress she was mending.

Less than five minutes later, I stood outside the gate to my house. Father's sheep looked like tiny flecks of white scattered across the sloping hills of our land.

I lifted the latch on the fence. Patches leapt forward and wedged himself between my legs, barking loudly in the direction of the house. No one could get him to shut up once he started barking. I dropped the latch, wondering why he was so worked up. That's when I noticed a car parked in the center of our front yard. I'd never seen it before. It was one of those compact city vehicles — I couldn't imagine someone driving it through the Highlands of Scotland.

I pushed open the screen door to the living room. At that moment, a wave of perfume hit me. The scent made the hairs on the back of my neck stand up.

"Uh-oh," I mumbled, realizing it was already too late to turn back.

Widow Rozenkratz, the superintendent of the schools, stared at me with her cold eyes. William Shuster, the barber's son, claimed that she'd been born a widow. I'd only seen her a couple of times during my life, but that was more than enough for me. Yet there she was, perched on an armchair in our living room, sitting in front of my mother and father.

Dad was wearing his work overalls — and a huge frown. He looked more disappointed than angry. Mom, on the other hand, looked like a pot that was about to boil over.

17

"Finley, come in," Mom said. "Keep Patches outside, please."

I had to shove Patches with my foot to get him to leave. After I closed the door, he sat with his nose pressed against the screen, growling quietly in the direction of the widow.

"Hello, Finley," Widow Rozenkratz said. "I imagine you know why I'm here."

"Not really," I lied, forcing myself to take a step forward. I'd learned long ago that adults were more likely to believe what you said if you didn't back away during an interrogation.

"How was school today?" my mother asked, but it didn't sound like a question.

I looked at my father and saw that his arms were crossed tightly over his chest. It looked like he was trying to keep something in that wanted to escape. I saw that his boots were still covered in mud. This was the worst sign of all: Mom had let him inside the house with his work boots on, which could only mean the worst.

"Well?" my mother asked.

I hesitated. It was obvious that they had found out about my trips to the river. At that point, coming clean was the best option for me since I couldn't lie my way out of it.

"I didn't go to school today," I said.

"And why not?" Mom asked.

I looked outside, thinking of the sun, the racing clouds, the azure skies that surrounded Applecross. "Because it's such a beautiful day," I said with a smile.

The widow's bony fingers grasped a notebook. The pages rustled as she flipped through it dramatically. "Counting today," she said, "your unexcused absences amount to seventy-one."

I shrugged. "It's been a really nice spring," I said.

"Shut up, Finley," my father said. I froze, avoiding eye contact.

My father looked into the widow's eyes. "Can anything be done about this?" he asked.

"I'm afraid not, Mr. McPhee," she said. "Your son's absences have piled up, and his grades weren't particularly high even before his absences began."

"But," I said, trailing off. I realized that none of them would care that I'd gotten a B in English that year.

The widow checked her notebook again. "Finley was barely passing most of his classes," she said. "That is, while he was still attending school."

"We honestly had no idea," my mother said. I saw that her anger had been transformed into embarrassment. I started to feel guilty. "We've always trusted Finley."

I opened my mouth to speak but said nothing. I realized that my case was over. At that point, I was just a guilty criminal waiting to hear my sentence.

"Do not fret too much, Mrs. McPhee," the widow said. "A lot of students have had to repeat a grade or two. In some cases, it can turn out to have a positive effect on the child."

"Yes, a good thing, of course," my father muttered. His voice sounded like a knife sharpening against a grindstone.

"It'll be a good opportunity for Finley to examine his behavior," the widow said. "It will be a pity if Finley doesn't begin to take his studies more seriously — his teachers tell me that he's a very bright boy."

My father nodded. "A very bright boy," he said, "who also needs a push in the right direction."

At that precise moment, Patches began to howl in the way he did when someone stepped on his tail.

"Get out of the way, Patches!" I heard my brother Doug say. He entered the living room, slamming the screen door behind him.

One by one, he stared at the four of us with his blank smile. As usual, he didn't have the slightest clue what was happening. "What's the deal?" he said in his booming voice. "Did someone die, or something?"

I always felt so small whenever Doug entered the room. I wished I could become invisible.

"Not yet," Mom said, glaring at me. "They're failing your brother at school."

Doug looked at me in a strange way. He appeared to be marveling at the fact that we actually had something in common.

"Really?" he said. He came over and ruffled my hair. "Cool."

"Not cool," my father muttered. It seemed to take him a lot of effort to stand. "Thank you for coming all the way here in person to see us, Mrs. Rozenkratz."

They shook hands.

"Just doing my job," the widow said.

"I imagine there wouldn't be any reason for Finley to attend these last few days of school, would there?" Dad asked.

The widow shook her head. "I'm afraid not, Mr. McPhee."

My father nodded slowly. "Shake hands with Mrs. Rozenkratz," my father ordered. I quickly took her hand and moved it up and down like a robot.

"We'll see you next year then, Finley," the widow said, forcing a smile.

Perhaps she felt sorry about the whole situation. Or

maybe she somehow knew what was going to happen over the next few days. I like to believe that I would have gotten to know the Lily family even if I hadn't failed school that year, but I guess I'll never know for sure.

The Widow Rozenkratz left the living room, leaving us in an embarrassed silence. When we heard the engine of her compact car start, Dad turned his back to me while Mom stormed off to the kitchen.

Doug was the only one to speak. "So what's for dinner?"

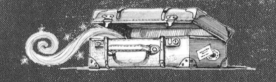

Chapter
THREE

THE REVEREND,
VOLUNTEERING, &
A SPRAINED ANKLE

I'm not going to tell you much about the rest of the day. I received a long scolding from Dad, then another one from Mom. Then they sent me to my bedroom without dinner and didn't even let Patches come up with me. He lay on the grass beneath my window instead, curled up underneath the beech tree.

I stretched out on my bed, letting thoughts race through my head. They weren't happy thoughts. I knew that I wouldn't be able to do whatever I wanted from now on, but that just meant I'd have to be more careful about covering my tracks. But then I wondered if I'd maybe taken things too far.

These thoughts ran through my head until it was

dark outside. I still hadn't made up my mind by then, but I did realize I didn't want to be treated like a little kid anymore.

Before heading to bed, my father knocked on my door. He was the only one who ever bothered to knock — Mom and Doug just barged right in.

I sat up and tried my best to look apologetic but not upset. "Come in," I said.

Dad opened the door but didn't step inside. "We've made sacrifices to send you to school, Finley," he said, picking up right where he'd left off earlier. "Your mother and I are struggling financially, even with your brother helping us keep on top of things."

"Dad, I'm sorry," I said. "I'd be happy to work with you and Doug —"

"No, you wouldn't be happy," my father interrupted. "After a summer of working, you'd be miserable — and you know it."

I knew he was right. To me, sheep were the dumbest, most boring animals in the whole world. Except for Doug, of course.

"We've made a lot of sacrifices for you," Dad repeated, "and this is how you pay us back. We knew right away that your brother wasn't cut out for college, but I thought you were different." He let the last sentence hang in the

air for a while. "I'm taking you to see Reverend Prospero tomorrow."

Then he left without waiting for a response.

I ran to the window. "Patches! Did you hear what they're going to do to me? They're taking me to Reverend Prospero!"

But the little traitor had already deserted his spot beneath my window. In the distance, I could see my dog chasing sheep happily in the moonlight.

That was the longest night of my life. I lay awake with my eyes open, listening to the whispering wind outside my window. Eventually I fell asleep only to be awoken by my mother at the crack of dawn.

"On your feet," she said. "Come on, lazy bones."

She literally pushed me out of bed, marched me to the bathroom, and pointed to the bath already filled with steaming water. On one side was a towel, on the other was my best suit — the one I wore to church. I cringed.

"You have fifteen minutes to get ready!" Mom said.

If I refused, I knew she would just push me into the tub with my clothes still on and wash me herself like I was a baby.

Ten minutes later, I sat at the kitchen table. The water in my bath had been so hot that I felt like I'd been skinned alive. My stomach was grumbling. Dad was

reading the sports page of the newspaper. He didn't speak.

"Hey, Einstein!" Doug said, sitting down across from me.

I didn't reply. My brother had made himself a mountain of scrambled eggs and was now pouring honey and mustard over it simultaneously. I was so hungry that I would've eaten that disgusting concoction. Instead, my mother gave me toast with jelly and some scrambled eggs, which I hated. But I didn't complain.

I quickly ate my breakfast, trying my best to ignore Doug's finger-tapping as he listened to his headphones. I just sat and waited nervously for whatever would come next.

My father rustled his newspaper and slapped it on the table. "Let's go," he said to me. Then he turned to face my brother. "Take those things out of your ears when you're at the table, Doug."

Dad and I climbed into the front seat of the van. Patches sat between us. As soon as we started moving, Patches scampered over my dress pants and stuck his nose out the window to let the rushing air tickle his ears.

I let him stay that way, but I held his collar so that he wouldn't fall out.

Soon, the small houses of Applecross came into view.

"Why do we have to go see Reverend Prospero?" I asked my father.

He kept staring straight ahead. "I asked him to find you a job this summer," he said.

"A job?" I said. "Why can't I work with you at the farm? Yesterday you said that you needed my help."

Dad parked the van in front of the church. He turned to stare straight at me. "Like I said last night, you'd probably enjoy yourself working at the farm for one summer," he said bitterly. "So I've asked the reverend to find you a job that you won't enjoy at all."

Dad climbed out of the van and slammed the door shut. "That way, maybe next time you'll think twice before wasting our money — and your life."

I felt like someone had punched me in the gut. I slowly climbed out of the van, gently closed the door, and followed my father toward the church.

Reverend Prospero was the village pastor. He'd baptized everyone in town, taken confession from all those who wished to confess, married every couple who wanted to get married, and had spoken the last rites for anyone who was dying. He lived in the parsonage behind the church with Ms. Finla, his housekeeper. She was probably the only person in Applecross who was older than Reverend Prospero.

My father led me toward the parsonage. As we passed between the house and the church, I saw the shadow of the Reverend rise before me. His fiery eyes burned into mine.

The reverend was a giant. His muscular arms and shoulders seemed better suited for a construction worker than a pastor. He'd been a chaplain in the army for a war or two. I couldn't remember which ones, but I could easily imagine him leading a troop of soldiers under enemy fire while playing the bagpipes.

He had a commanding voice and a stern attitude. He was fond of saying, "To save your soul, you have to beat it into submission." The only thing that prevented him from being completely intimidating was his huge mustache and the tufts of hair that sprouted from his ears. He was bald everywhere else.

Meb McCameron once told me that Reverend Prospero had a mysterious tattoo on his shoulder. She claimed she'd seen it when he was being measured for his new vestments at her shop. I was curious to find out if it was true, but I wasn't about to ask the reverend.

"So, Finley McPhee," Reverend Prospero boomed. "What have you done this time?"

It wasn't the first time I'd been dragged into his presence. About a year ago, Jackie Turbine, Sammy

Monkfish, and I had broken Mr. Everett's window with a rugby ball. Mr. Everett's house was right behind the field, and Jackie Turbine had the best kick in the entire village, so it wasn't really our fault. Although we probably should have stopped playing after we'd broken the first window. And maybe we shouldn't have trampled through Mrs. Gordon's garden while fleeing from Mr. Everett.

That time, Reverend Prospero said that it was just a matter of boys being boys. He made me and Sammy weed Mrs. Gordon's garden for a month, and he ordered Jackie to clean the moss off all the gravestones at the cemetery.

"Well, Finley?" the reverend asked. "Why are you here?"

"I spent too much time fishing, Reverend," I said.

Reverend Prospero laughed heartily. "Instead of going to school, you mean," he said. "So what are we going to do with you?"

"It's up to you, Reverend," I said. I may have been smiling, but I was also sweating through my best suit.

"What are you good at?" he asked.

I thought for a moment. I knew how to fish pretty well, and I had a sharp eye for finding things that washed up on the beach. I could read and write pretty well, and I loved American comic books. I could sprint through the forests in the winter and through the fields in summer. In fact, when I went running with Patches, sometimes I even beat him in a race. I also knew how to recognize the entrances to the Little People's kingdom, and I knew all sorts of sneaky shortcuts through the village.

But those weren't the types of things the reverend was looking for, so I simply shrugged.

"So you aren't good at anything?" the reverend said. It sounded more like a challenge than a question.

I frowned. My father gave me a sharp shove forward, making me almost fall over. "I leave him in your capable hands, Prospero," Dad said. "I need to get back to the farm."

The two men nodded at each other as if they had worked out everything beforehand. I imagined them talking to each other on the phone while I had been locked in my room, discussing the situation in that clipped, concise way that grown men use when they discuss important stuff.

"Follow me," the reverend said, leading the way.

Because I was younger than fourteen, I couldn't legally work. There was a law against the abuse of child labor, or something like that. But that fact wasn't going to stop the reverend from forcing me to "give him a hand" here and there for free wherever he needed help.

"Besides," he often said, "giving back to the community is the traditional Scottish cure for laziness."

The first day, I had to work in the supermarket. They put me in the warehouse, where I unloaded the packages, and then lifted them onto the shelves. At first it seemed like it might be fun, but it didn't turn out that way. More and more packages arrived as the day went on, and they all had to be placed on the shelves in a specific order. Apparently there was a particular way of shelving the items, but I didn't get it. I had no idea so many products could fill the back storeroom of a small market, or that so many people could come in asking for so many different things.

By midmorning, my shoulders were aching. Mr. Cullen, the owner, hadn't spoken to me until then. He saw that my work rate had slowed, so he pointed at a stool by the register. "Take a break from shelving while I go to the bank," he said. "If anyone comes in, tell them I'll be back shortly."

As soon as he'd left, I went to get a popsicle from the freezer. I ate it quickly so he wouldn't see me with it when he came back. Just then, a man I'd never seen before entered the shop. He looked like a rock star — really tall and thin with blond, shaggy hair and a spaced-out expression.

He glanced left and right as if trying to figure out where he was. "Do you have any pizza?" he asked. I pointed to the appropriate shelf. He walked over to examine them. A moment later, he picked up three pizzas and carried them to the register and set them on the counter.

The man rifled through his pockets only to find that both of them were empty. "Sorry about this," he said, "but I seem to have forgotten my wallet at home. Can I come back later to pay for these?"

I looked outside in the direction of the bank to see if Mr. Cullen was on his way back, but he wasn't. I had to make a managerial decision.

"Okay," I said to the stranger. "But you will come back later to pay, right?"

"Yes, of course I will," he said. "Thanks, kid."

Later, when I told Mr. Cullen about the situation, he simply pointed at a sign on the wall that read "NO CREDIT. NO EXCEPTIONS!" He sent me back to Reverend Prospero.

★ ★ ★

The next day, I began to "volunteer" at the post office. I stayed there a whole week, moving and sorting mail. Again I was surprised by the sheer quantity of letters and packages that the people of Applecross sent and received.

With email and smartphones and computers, I'd figured that snail mail was dead and gone.

I enjoyed my time there for the most part. At the end of that week, some good news came my way. Jules, the village mailman, had sprained an ankle while running away from the McBlack sheepdog. He re-enacted the entire incident, gesturing wildly and even using different voices. My new colleagues seemed quite shocked by the whole series of events. "No one," Jules stated, "should have to deliver mail to the McBlacks."

There was a lot of local gossip that supported his perspective. The McBlacks had a reputation for being troublemakers. Their house had been given the nickname Eerie House even if there was nothing frightening about it, apart from maybe the headless statue in the front yard. People loved to gossip about the supposedly ferocious McBlack sheepdog, but it had always seemed nice enough to me.

Regardless, Jules had definitely sprained his ankle. He had it propped up on a chair, covered in ice packs.

"This is a bad situation, Jules," said the lady who sat behind the counter. "If you can't ride your bike, then who is going to deliver mail on your route?"

In a split second, all eyes were on me. It took me even less than that to graciously accept my new job.

THE BICYCLE,
THE MAILBAG, &
MAGICAL INK

School officially closed its doors for summer vacation on the second Saturday in June. It was also the day when the names and grades were posted, along with the names of those who had failed (only me).

Meanwhile, I was out pedaling the mailman's bicycle. Patches was scurrying behind me, determined not to let me get too far ahead of him. When the route took me up a hill, I pedaled even harder. Jules's bike felt like it might break at any moment, which would have been a disaster. After all, it was my first day being a mailman.

I had the mailbag slung over my shoulder as I rode. I hadn't sorted the mail before leaving like Jules usually

did. Instead, I pulled out one letter at a time from the mailbag, read the address, and then took off to deliver it.

It was actually kind of fun. Everyone, especially the people living on the farms, thanked me for bringing them their mail. Several families invited me in for lemonade and kept their dogs outside so they wouldn't fight with Patches. During the few weeks I delivered their mail, I learned more about the families of Applecross than I had in the previous thirteen years. After that experience, the village of Applecross seemed both larger and smaller at the same time.

As I traveled from house to house, my dog happily marked his territory at every stop we made, completely untroubled by the many growling sheepdogs we passed by. Around one in the afternoon, Patches had started to pant as he trotted along behind me. I was getting pretty tired myself, so I decided to deliver one last letter before taking my lunch break.

I remember the next few moments perfectly. I was biking on a small country road beside a long stretch of grass that was bordered by a stone wall. There was a gnarled oak tree by the side of the road that had a dense array of twisted branches. My watch read 1:13 p.m. exactly when I stopped my bike to pull the letter from my mailbag.

The envelope felt strange in my hands, almost as if it were alive. It was long, narrow, and had ornate handwriting that looked like it had been pressed with gold foil. The envelope had been sent from somewhere in London called The Imaginary Travelers Club. The letter was addressed to:

> *The Lily Family*
> *Enchanted Emporium*
> *36 Eggstones Heaven*
> *Reginald Bay, Applecross (Scotland)*

At first I thought it was a joke. I'd never heard of a Lily family who lived in Applecross, or a place called Eggstones Heaven, or even a Reginald Bay.

I noticed the letter had a strange scent, and it seemed to quiver in my hands. I tried to fold the envelope, but it wouldn't bend. It seemed to be made of something much stronger than paper despite the fact that it didn't seem to weigh anything at all. When I tilted the letter, it sounded like sand was falling from one end to the other.

"Like an hourglass," I murmured. I held the envelope up to the light, but I couldn't see anything inside it.

I sighed. "Let's go home for lunch, Patches," I said. "We'll have a better chance at cracking this case with full stomachs." Patches barked in agreement.

39

Lost in thought, I pedaled toward home at a leisurely pace, wondering about that mysterious letter.

I had no idea at the time, but delivering the mysterious envelope would prove to be much harder than I thought.

A BOTTLE
❦ of ❧
GOLDEN INK

Gold Pens

This magical ink allows one to send private information safely and securely. Upon writing an address in this special ink, the envelope is sealed with an invisible barrier that prevents nosy mailmen from tampering with it.

Applecross, Scotland

The Imaginary Travelers Club
London

Chapter
FIVE

A RED HOUSE,
A GREEN-EYED GIRL,
& MORE MYSTERIES

I sat down at the table across from my brother and mother. "Hey, Doug," I said. "Have you heard of a place called Reginald Bay?"

My brother stopped chewing for a moment. "Huh?" he asked.

"Reginald Bay?" I repeated, enunciating each syllable. "Have you heard of it?"

Doug just shrugged and continued chewing.

"Ask your father," Mom suggested. "When it comes to Scotland's geography, nobody knows more than he does."

It was true. Talking to my father about Scotland, you'd think he had traveled the country many times over

by the way he recognized every single place's name. Yet I never saw him look at an atlas or map. *The Imaginary Travelers Club should have addressed their letter to my dad, I* thought.

I found Dad leaning against the sheep pen while gazing over the gently rolling valleys. I was still a little nervous as I approached him, but not as much as I had been the previous week. Now that I had a job, in his eyes I was doing something useful instead of "wasting my time down by the river."

"Hey, dad," I said, "Have you heard of Reginald Bay?"

He seemed to think for a moment. *That's a good sign,* I thought. *It must mean he knows it.*

"Reginald, you say," he said, thinking out loud. "If it's the place I remember, it's no longer called by that name."

Dad pointed toward the northern coast of Applecross, a little way beyond the old mill. "Have you heard of the White Bay before?" he asked.

I nodded. "It got its name because of the light-colored pebbles on the shore."

Dad nodded. "There are a couple of coves in that area," he said. "There used to be an oak forest past a small promontory. Past that, there's a big beach with stones and rocks."

"You mean Burnt Beach?" I asked.

"That's the one," Dad said. "Once upon a time, before the oak trees were all burned down, they used to call it Reginald Bay."

"Why did they call it that?" I asked.

"That story is actually quite interesting," Dad said. He rubbed his chin. "It's an old shipwreck tale. A man named Reginald once crashed his ship there, so they named the place after him. You know what the people of Applecross are like — if something out of the ordinary happens, they name it after the event." Dad rolled his eyes.

"Well," I said, "I think a shipwreck kind of deserves a name."

"There have been dozens of shipwrecks in Scotland," Dad said with a wave of his hand. "Although that particular one was unusual, if I recall correctly — that Reginald guy's ship was painted completely red."

I nodded. Both of us silently regarded the rolling hills for a few moments. "Do you know where 36 Eggstones is?" I asked after I'd determined my father had finished speaking on the previous subject.

Dad shrugged. "Never heard of it," he said. "If it's near the Reginald Bay that I'm talking about, it's on the other side of Applecross — at least twenty minutes by bicycle."

"More like half an hour if Patches tags along," I said. For the first time in weeks, my father smiled at me.

★ ★ ★

I reached Reginald Bay early that afternoon. I was greeted by sunlight sparkling in a continuous stream of reflected light from the sea. By comparison, the outline of the isle of Skyle looked like a brooding sentry.

I followed the main road to a small path that led toward the blackened tree trunks of Burnt Beach. After a few minutes of pedaling, I emerged again among the rocks that formed the promontory.

I stopped at an arrow-shaped road sign that I'd never seen before. The direction it pointed seemed to change depending on which way you looked at it. "Not a very useful sign," I muttered to myself.

My dog barked. "What do you think, Patches?" I asked. "If we look at it from this side, it's telling us to go straight. But if we look at it from over here, it seems to be pointing down this path."

Patches barked toward the path, so I pedaled the bike in that direction. We passed a group of huge boulders arranged in a semicircle. I remember thinking that they looked like they'd been placed there by a giant. I didn't know it at the time, but that is exactly how they got there.

I followed the path around a turn and down a hill. Farther below, a few feet from me, I could see the waves breaking on the rocks. The path continued about halfway up the coast to a small house that I had never seen before.

I blinked hard, surprised to see a house this far out from the village. It had a black, pointed roof with a large stone chimney poking out of it. The walls were bright red. There was a large window that made the house look kind of like a shop. On the top floor, there were a couple of smaller windows with open shutters and white frames.

Patches crouched in front of me and began to wag his tail, waiting for me to continue. I leaned the bicycle against one of the many oval-shaped stones scattered over the promontory and then began to walk down the path. There was a light breeze, so the only noise I heard was Patches trotting along beside me.

As I walked, my imagination began to play tricks on me. I had this weird feeling that I was being watched. A strange idea popped into my head that many tiny creatures were hiding behind the stones and spying on me. I scanned the area, but the only signs of life were seagulls perched on the nearby stones.

We passed one particularly large seagull that stared

at us without budging an inch from its spot. It had a curved beak that looked as sharp as a knife.

I drew the mailbag closer and tried to look more confident. "I wonder where number 36 is," I said, mostly to myself.

Then something weird happened — I swear I heard that creepy seagull say, "Down there." It seemed to be pointing at the red house with its beak.

I shook my head. I knew I must be hearing things. After all, seagulls are known for making shrill noises that can sound like human cries. Despite knowing that, my legs refused to move. Patches seemed calm as though nothing had happened.

I made myself turn around and stare at the seagull on its perch. It was looking at me as if to say, "Well? Are you going or not?"

I swallowed hard, drew the mailbag even closer to me, and walked on.

As I got closer, I saw the number 36 beside the door. Even though there were no other houses around, the red cottage was number 36. *Weird,* I thought.

I could have just left the package by the door and turned around to leave, but I didn't. To be honest, the place intrigued me. I was fascinated by the thousands of rocks and stones lying around, the noise of the sea and the seagulls, and the sun that was beginning to set behind the islands. I felt a great sense of peace while I stood there, kind of like the time I spent alone down by the river. It felt like magic. Maybe it was.

I looked around for a doorbell but couldn't find one. I looked for a knocker, but there wasn't one of those, either. So I tried to walk around the side of the house, but that wasn't possible because it'd been built directly into the cliff, and it was surrounded by dense bushes of Butcher's Broom with its prickly bunches of scarlet berries. I didn't realize it at the time, but even that detail was strange since Butcher's Broom produces its berries in a completely different time of the year. As it turns out, that was only one of many oddities I'd missed.

I walked back to the front door. I sighed and shrugged at Patches. "Looks like no one's home," I said. I turned my back to the red house and gazed at the endless rocks that had been shifted and eroded by the wind. Suddenly, Patches barked so loudly that it made me jump.

"What's up, pal?" I asked, crouching down to pet him. Patches's tail was bolt upright and he was pushing his nose against the base of the front door. I knelt down to look for myself. Just then, I heard what sounded like dozens of complicated bolts unlocking. A moment later, the door opened a crack. A pale white hand with long tapered nails emerged. Then an arm appeared, and then a shoulder, until finally I met Aiby Lily for the very first time.

I must have looked pretty strange kneeling on her doorstep with my jaw wide open, because she asked me, "Are you okay?"

She was tall and slender with very long arms and legs. She had a flowing cascade of straight black hair. Her eyes were a striking lime green. Her clothes were nice, but it looked like she'd opened her closet and let various pieces of clothing just fall onto her. She wore two sweaters, jeans, a fancy belt buckle, and a pair of funny-looking, striped socks. She looked ridiculous and fabulous at the same time.

And she was easily the most beautiful girl I'd ever seen.

"I think you're strangling him," Aiby said, pointing at Patches.

She was right. I'd been so surprised by her appearance that I'd been accidentally throttling my dog's neck. I let him go and rose to my feet in one quick, smooth movement.

"Um, hi," I said, and then finally closed my mouth. I pointed to the cliff face behind us. "Sorry about the intrusion, but I didn't think anyone was home."

She ran her hands through her hair and laughed. "That's okay," she said. Then she added in a low voice, "The truth is, I'd fallen asleep." She stretched and covered her mouth to stifle a yawn, highlighting the freckles and dimples at the edges of her mouth.

"What brings you here?" she asked, tilting her head. "We haven't opened our shop yet."

"Huh?" I said.

"Who are you?" she said.

I realized that I hadn't introduced myself. "My name is Finley McPhee. It begins with an 'F.' I'm the mailman. Well, I'm not really the mailman — Jules is. But today I'm taking his place. This is Patches, my dog."

"You're the mailman?" she asked.

I nodded. "For now."

I searched through the mailbag and took out the letter that had sent me there. I read the address out loud, then asked her, "Is that you?"

"I'm not the whole Lily family," she said with a grin, "but yes, I'm one of them." She offered her hand. "I'm Aiby Lily. Pleasure to meet you."

As I shook her hand, a surge of heat traveled up my arm to my neck. "Nice to meet you too, Aiby," I said. "So I guess this is yours."

I handed Aiby the envelope with the gold lettering.

She gave it a quick glance and then tucked it into one of the many pockets in her jeans.

"Thanks," she said with a smile. "This letter is a big deal for me. It's the first one I've received here."

"Really?" I said. "What's it about?"

Aiby frowned and stared at her feet. I wondered if she'd quickly tucked the letter into her jeans because it was supposed to be a secret.

I blushed. "You don't have to tell me. I found a message in a bottle on the beach once," I lied, trying to change the subject.

"Really?" she asked.

"Yep," I said proudly.

Aiby let out a musical laugh. "What was the message?"

I winked. "It's a secret."

She grinned. "My dad likes that kind of stuff," she said. "Finding rare items, hunting for rocks, things like that."

"How long have you lived here?" I asked.

"We just got here, actually," Aiby said.

"I knew it."

"What did you know?"

I blushed. "Well, I've never seen you in the village before, and it's not like there are thousands of people passing through. Actually, I've never even seen your house before today. It's very . . ." Aiby followed my gaze to the red wooden walls of the cottage, waiting for me to finish speaking. "It's very red," I finally said.

"I think it's cool," Aiby said. "I mean, the color is weird, but I like it. You can see it from far out at sea, which was helpful."

I raised an eyebrow.

"It took me and my dad forever to find it," she explained.

"To find it?" I asked.

"We didn't know where the house was located," Aiby said. "At one point, we thought we'd made a mistake and stopped looking. We almost went home. Then, all of a sudden, there it was — my great-great-grandfather's red house."

"Your grandfather built it?" I asked, vaguely recalling my father's story about the shipwrecked captain and his red boat.

Aiby looked at me intently with her big, green eyes. "My great-great-grandfather," she said. "Or something like that. I'm not very good with family trees."

I scratched my head. "Me neither," I said. "But that means your great-great-grandfather lived in Applecross."

She giggled. "Of course he did," she said. "Are you making fun of me, Finley?"

53

I blushed. "No!" I said. "I only asked because I wanted to know if —"

I heard a loud crash behind me. I turned to look. Beyond the inlet, a huge slab of rock had fallen onto the bicycle, knocking it to the ground.

"Oh, no!" I cried. "Jules's bike!"

We both dashed down the path toward the bicycle. I lifted it upright and tried to spin the wheels. The front wheel was fine, but the back wheel wouldn't move. The boulder had damaged the chain.

"Look at that!" I said. "How am I going to get back to the village now?"

Aiby crouched beside me. She grabbed a pedal, then looked me in the eyes. "If you promise not to tell anyone," she said, "I can fix it for you."

"Why would I tell anyone?" I asked.

"Do you promise?" she asked.

I nodded.

"Turn around," she said.

"Huh?" I said.

She slipped a hand under her shirt and took out a brass pendant that was shaped like a spider. It looked different than the jewelry most girls wore.

"Turn around," Aiby insisted.

I turned to look out to sea. Behind me, I heard Aiby

press the brass spider against the bicycle's chain. I heard a strange clicking noise, then a crack. Then I heard the sound of metal legs tapping rapidly. Then I heard her whisper something like, "Magic word: character."

Patches began to growl. I was so confused by what was happening that I didn't turn around or even speak.

Aiby let out a little cough. "There," she said, turning me around. "Your bike's as good as new."

I checked the chain. It whirred around perfectly. "What did you do?" I asked.

"Nothing," she murmured, lowering her sparkling eyes.

"What do you mean?" I asked.

She tilted her head. A wisp of black hair fell across her eyes. "No one can know everything, Finley."

The sudden sensation of rain falling on my head made her strange statement seem profound. We both looked up at the oncoming rain clouds. Aiby sprinted toward her house.

"Wait," I said.

"Thank you for the letter, Finley McPhee," she shouted without turning around. "Enjoy the rest of the afternoon!"

"Wait, Aiby! Where are you going?" I asked.

It was obvious where she was going — inside. I

wasn't feeling particularly smart that day. "May I see you again?" I called out.

Her answer was a laugh that sounded like tinkling glass. A moment later, she disappeared behind the wooden door of the red house.

The sky darkened and the drops fell even harder. It seemed appropriate that it was raining so hard — I already felt like I'd been struck by a huge bolt of lightning. I looked around at the burnt tree trunks that used to be a forest. Perhaps lightning had struck the same spot twice — once for the forest, and now for me and for Aiby.

"We'll see each other again," I said to myself, but I wasn't convinced.

I sighed and pushed the bicycle through the Burnt Beach. My dog followed faithfully. "Looks like it's just the two of us again, eh, Patches?"

Patches wagged his tail and barked.

FIX-IT SPIDER

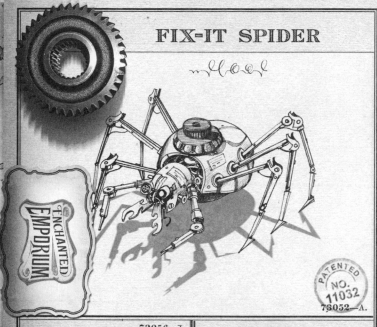

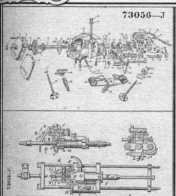

PATENTED
NO.
11032
73052—A.

73056—J

The **FIX-IT SPIDER** is one of forty mechanical miniatures created by legendary craftsman Omar Ich'Bin-Kayann. Each of the forty automatons specializes in a different mechanical art, but the rest remain hidden in Ali Baba's secret treasure trove.

Chapter
SIX

THE RIDDLE,
THE PIZZA THIEF, &
THE MAGICAL PANTS

ater that evening, I strolled lazily along the soft, wet beach, leaving a long trail of shallow footprints behind me. The only creatures around were mosquitos, but they didn't seem particularly interested in me.

There was just enough light to illuminate the edge of the water. I saw ribbons of algae, branches, shells, and other debris that had washed in from the sea. I'd brought my backpack with me like I always did whenever I went treasure hunting. Normally, I'd carefully comb the beach in search of rare finds, but that evening I just couldn't stop thinking about Aiby.

I had counted every minute that had passed since

we parted ways. In that time, I'd thought about almost nothing else. I was still a little overwhelmed by the fact that Aiby had repaired Jules's bicycle with a magical robot spider while speaking strange words.

While I walked and wondered about the day's events, Patches stopped to sniff at something on the shore. I figured he'd soon yelp because a crab had pinched his nose, and then bark at it in revenge.

And he did yelp. And then he barked. I dug my hands deeper into my pockets and kept walking, smiling to myself. I liked it when things happened the way I expected them to. It made me feel like I actually understood how the world worked sometimes.

I reached the end of the beach where the white sand gave way to black rocks. Patches still hadn't given up his mad pursuit of the crab. I glanced upward at the stars in the sky. They were so beautiful that it made the grating cloud of mosquitoes sound more like violins in an orchestra tuning up for a performance.

"Patches, give up already," I said. "And get over here, will ya?"

I retraced my steps to the spot where my stubborn little friend had been pinched. I found him barking and growling at a pile of black seaweed. His muzzle was

placed stubbornly between his front paws and his tail was raised in the air.

"What's wrong with you, boy?" I asked.

I gave a cautious kick at the pile of seaweed near Patches and realized there was something underneath.

"What's that?" I muttered, crouching on the damp sand.

I recognized what the object was, but I couldn't believe my eyes. "No way!" I said, and then repeated it probably a dozen more times.

At every low tide in the last five years, I had trawled the beaches of Applecross hoping to find something like this. And now that I had finally come across an actual message in a bottle, all I could do was stare at it.

In a burst of uncharacteristic courage, Patches nipped at the bottle. With great care, I dislodged it from the sand and held it up to my eyes. I studied it against the light, shifting it back and forth in front of the moon.

"There's no doubt about it, Patches!" I said. "We've just discovered a message in a bottle!"

The bottle looked normal enough, but the label had long since worn away. The bottom of the bottle had an inscription that read, "Murano Brothers – Sea Couriers – Always Riding the Crest of a Wave."

The scroll of paper inside was dry and safe due to a strong cork that appeared to be sealed with wax. I pulled out my pocket knife and popped the cork off. Slowly, I tilted the bottle until the sheet of paper slipped into the palm of my hand. I carefully unrolled it to reveal a written message. I read it aloud: "Five people were crossing the land, all dressed in black. One was a woman, the other four were men. They got caught in a sudden storm. Rain poured down and lightning struck. The four men fled for cover, but they arrived at their destination wet. The woman did not run, but she stayed dry. Now I ask you this question: why did the woman stay dry?"

It was a riddle! I re-read it a dozen more times. Then I checked inside the bottle to see if there was anything I'd missed, but I found nothing.

I couldn't make my mind up whether to be happy or disappointed. On one hand, I had finally found a message in a bottle. I could just imagine waving it in front of Doug's face to show him that I wasn't as crazy as he said I was — that bottles with messages really did exist.

On the other hand, I could imagine what he would say after he read the message. I imagined it would be

something like, "That's great, Viper, you found a useless riddle. Who cares?"

And honestly, he would have been right. Why would anyone put a message like that one out to sea?

I wondered if it was just someone playing a joke on me. After all, it was a pretty huge coincidence that I'd found it on the same day that I'd mentioned messages in bottles to Aiby. Even though she'd seemed to be kind of playful, I didn't think she'd be the type to try a practical joke like this.

I thought about the message, Aiby, and the bottle while I walked all the way up the road that led from the beach to Baelanch Ba. At that point, I started to try to solve the riddle. *Four men and one woman, all dressed in black, got caught in the rain,* I recalled. *The men ran, but she didn't. Yet she stayed dry while they got soaked.*

Where did the men run? I wondered. *And why does the color of their clothing even matter?*

Just then, I saw the man with the blond hair who had taken the pizzas from the supermarket the week before. He was walking swiftly down the middle of the road toward me. He wore black clothing and carried a bouquet of flowers. The silvery moonlight gave his blond hair a ghostly halo. Not that ghosts have halos, but that was the thought that was going through my mind at the time.

Before Patches knew what was happening, I grabbed him by the collar and pulled him behind one of the standing stones along the edge of the road.

I kept my dog's muzzle closed with my hands. "Promise not to bark, okay?" I said, looking him directly in the eyes.

Patches whimpered, indicating that he understood. I slid myself around the stone to get a better view of the road. As I did, I heard the message in the bottle tinkle in my backpack. *There are way too many strange things happening in Applecross today,* I thought wearily.

That's when I realized that the blond guy wasn't actually walking on the road. His legs weren't even moving, yet he was traveling quite quickly. In fact, you couldn't even see his feet because his pants were so long that they covered his shoes. The closer he got, the more it looked like his pants were doing the walking for him, as weird as that sounds.

I felt like I was in shock. Patches looked just as confused as I was. We continued to watch the man come closer while hiding behind the stone. As he finally passed by us, I could clearly see that his pants were carrying him toward the village. I blinked hard, then looked again. His pants were definitely moving for him!

"You saw it too, didn't you, Patches?" I whispered as soon as the man was out of earshot. "And why is he holding a bunch of flowers?"

Any other person would have just run home, locked himself in his bedroom, and hid under the covers. But not me, and not my dog. In fact, I'm the last person who would flee from scary stuff.

I scratched my head. I didn't know what to believe at that point. I decided the best course of action was to keep my mind open to all possibilities, as strange as some of them were.

Patches whimpered. "Don't worry," I said, trying to reassure my dog. "We won't let him get away without making him answer a few of our questions."

I straddled the bicycle while the blond man and his magical pants glided farther away. I looked down again at Patches and noticed for the first time how tired my dog looked from following me around all day.

"Okay," I said. I shook off my backpack and opened it up in front of Patches. "Hop in. But when I put you back on my shoulders, don't wiggle around and act all crazy like you usually do. Got it?"

So, with Patches on my shoulders and the pedals beneath my feet, I chased after the blond pizza thief and his self-propelling pants.

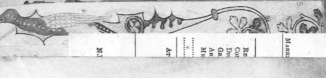

Self-Propelling Pants

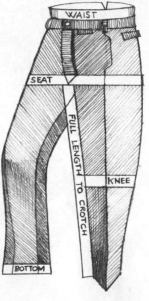

WAIST

SEAT

FULL LENGTH TO CROTCH

KNEE

BOTTOM

INCORPORATED
GENTLEMEN'S TAILORS

An ancient tailor weaved a restless
spirit into the cloth of these pants,
making them propel their wearer wherever they
please. By applying a mixture of Mandrake Oil and
Mercury Fumes, one can grant these pants an eerie
glow that is sure to turn heads.

EMPORIUM

Chapter
SEVEN

SNORING,
THE CEMETERY,
& GHOSTS

The strange blond man floated through the deserted village. The shop lights were off, as were the lamps in the houses, but the luminous pants somehow bathed the street in a phosphorescent glow. The only other light was an intermittent bright flash from Seamus's garage. It looked like a torch flame was being used, meaning Seamus was probably working on one of his many satellite television devices.

The floating stranger turned toward the center of the village and, to my surprise, stopped a few paces from the church. I hid myself behind the corner of a narrow alleyway so that I could watch him undetected.

Not even a sliver of light emanated from the church. The building was enveloped in mist, which was unusual for that time of year.

Patches growled softly toward the end of the alleyway. I turned around to see what he'd growled at, but nothing was there. Then someone closed a door. I heard the sound of distant footsteps. A cough echoed through the deserted streets. I wasn't able to locate the source of any of the sounds.

When I finally turned back to the floating man, he had disappeared.

"Patches, he's gone!" I said.

I leaned the bicycle against a wall and slowly approached the church. As we walked, I kept my eyes on the courtyard and Patches covered the rear.

When I passed the front door of the parsonage, I could hear loud snoring coming from the top floor. I figured it was Reverend Prospero, but after walking a few more steps I heard a similar noise and realized that snoring was also coming from Ms. Finla's room. I found their simultaneous snoring to be sort of reassuring, so I continued onward.

As I turned the corner, I saw the man in the self-propelling pants hovering over the damp grass where the

gravestones were. I watched him from a safe distance, trying to fight back the shivers from seeing a magical man wandering a cemetery at night.

The moon had disappeared behind some clouds, making the pants' glow the only source of light. As the eerie light flickered among the dark graves, my courage began to desert me. After all the strange things that had happened to me that day, you'd think I'd be ready for anything. But you'd be wrong. I kept my distance.

The man seemed to be searching for something around the gravestones. He searched through the weeds that covered the cemetery. He read some of the half-eroded epitaphs on the stones.

When he proceeded deeper into the cemetery, I walked along the wall so that I could keep him in sight without him seeing me. The man just continued to scan the ground for something.

At that moment, Aiby's words about messages in bottles popped into my head: "My dad likes that kind of thing," she had said. *Weird,* I thought. *Why did I think of that just now?*

When I finally snapped back to focus, I saw that the floating man had disappeared again! I swore under my breath, then quickly moved along the wall to see

if I could find him again. Just then, I heard a voice in the distance. As I moved toward the sound, I heard the rustling of paper. It sounded just like the tissue that you wrap around flowers.

That must be him, I thought. But before I could move any closer, a loud cracking sound rang out through the cemetery, illuminating the area with a brilliant blue-white light. As my eyes came back into focus, I saw a blue flame was burning directly above a gravestone. It looked like the head of a giant match. The thought made me feel dizzy. I leaned against a nearby gravestone and tried to understand what I was seeing.

Patches was trying to wriggle out of my backpack, so I reached over my shoulder and gently stroked his ears to calm him down. Then I gathered my courage and took a few cautious first steps, trying not to walk over the graves that were closest to me.

As soon as I could see the blue light again, I hid myself behind an imposing stone cross. Atop the cross was an even more imposing angel with outspread wings. I felt a cold surge of panic crawl up my spine, but I somehow managed to ignore it.

The strange man was standing before two crooked gravestones adjacent to each other. The blue light flickered above them. The man had placed the bouquet of flowers on the ground in front of the graves. He had his hands clasped together as he murmured some strange words. Despite the silence of the night, I still couldn't make out a word from where I hid.

Rigid as a statue, I tiptoed past a few more graves to get even closer. A twig snapped under my shoe. I froze, certain that the man had heard me. But he just continued to stare at the tombstones and murmur quietly.

When I reached a second cross, I could hear a few of the words the man was speaking. "You can't remember where you placed it?" he said. And then, "No, it isn't in the cellar. I already checked there. Twice."

Who was this nutcase talking to in a cemetery in the middle of the night? I wondered. The thought that he might be talking to himself didn't make me feel any better.

I could feel Patches's claws scratching against the inside of my backpack in an attempt to free himself. I slipped the backpack off my shoulders and carefully set it on the ground, but he continued to wiggle around inside the bag.

"The chimney, you say?" the strange man muttered. "Where in the chimney?"

I dug my nails into the moss-covered cross and slowly raised my eyes over its base to get a better view of the action.

Once I saw what was happening, I froze from my fingers all the way down to my toes. The blue flame that fluttered above the graves had taken the form of a face. It had empty sockets for eyes, and its enormous mouth expanded and contracted as though the face was talking. I didn't hear a voice coming from the mouth, but the floating man seemed to be able to hear and understand it just fine.

While I was paralyzed with fear, Patches managed to free himself from the backpack. With a burst of energy, he dashed toward the man, howling what sounded like a doggy battle cry.

While my dog was far from intimidating, and always a major pain, I had to admire his courage. In the relative darkness, Patches seemed quite a bit bigger than he actually was.

As Patches neared the blue flame, it quickly melted away. Just as rapidly, the mysterious stranger vanished into thin air. One moment the man was standing in front of the two, crooked gravestones, and the next he had disappeared.

Patches landed on top of the bouquet of flowers that lay on the grass. He looked up in confusion for a moment, then promptly began to tear the flowers to shreds.

My knuckles ached from clutching the cross during the ghostly encounter, or whatever it had been. I ran over to Patches to find that he'd scattered flowers all over the cemetery.

"Congratulations, Patches," I said. "You defeated the deadly bouquet of flowers." He continued to growl even after I lifted him off the ground.

One of the clouds shifted, allowing a sliver of moonlight to fall across the cemetery. That was when I saw the names that were engraved on the two gravestones in front of me: Charlotte and Reginald Lily.

That was the exact moment I realized that there's no such thing as a coincidence. I ran away from the graveyard in a mad sprint toward home.

I didn't stop running until the farmhouse door slammed behind me. I secured every single bolt and chain, then ran up to my bedroom and locked that door, too.

I jumped into bed still fully dressed and yanked the covers over myself with Patches curled up in a ball near

my feet. I spent most of the rest of the night waiting for my hands and feet to warm up, but no matter what I did they still felt like big blocks of ice.

I didn't sleep a wink that night.

SPIRIT POWDER

This **MAGICAL POWDER** is composed of two parts saltpetre, one part lazaria crystal, and one part dragon's breath. Its formula dates all the way back to the **Count of Cagliostro** in the **seventeenth century**. Dusting a gravesite with this powder enables you to briefly recall a spirit, allowing you to converse with it (if the spirit is willing to cooperate).

LAZARIA CRYSTAL

DEAD MAN TALKING

Chapter
EIGHT

PROSPERO,
A HISTORY LESSON,
& CASTLE RUINS

I went to see Reverend Prospero the next morning. I found him in the choir room, where he was working on the score for that evening's rehearsal.

"McPhee, what a pleasant surprise!" he said in his booming voice. "How are we doing?"

I muttered that everything was going fine at the post office.

"I must say, I've never seen Jules happier since he sprained his ankle!" the reverend said.

I wasn't surprised. Ever since I'd taken over his mail route, Jules had finally been able to dedicate himself to his favorite hobby: village gossip.

I helped the reverend sort through the hymnals and the sheet music. He played a few notes on the organ

79

to make sure it was in tune, and then read through the order of hymns prepared by the choirmaster. He grumbled when he saw the last piece. "I think I need to have a word with Mr. Fionnir," he said. "This really is too much. Has anyone ever heard of a church choir singing 'The Giants of the Sea?' It's bad enough that we sing about Oberon and Puck and all the rest of those pagan creatures!"

The reverend seemed angry, but he really wasn't. Like all good Scots, he'd long ago learned to be accepting of belief and superstition, religion and legend. Finding a balance between these spiritual differences came naturally to us.

When I finally managed to get a word in, I said, "Reverend, can I ask you something?"

"Of course you can."

"Have you ever heard of the Lily family in Applecross?"

"What's that you say?"

"The Lily family," I repeated, my voice shaking a little.

"Lily?" the reverend repeated. He seemed genuinely surprised to hear the name. "I have heard the family name before, but if memory serves me, there hasn't been

a Lily living here for over a hundred years. Perhaps even longer."

The reverend raised a bushy eyebrow in my direction. "Why do you ask?"

"Just curious," I said.

"Well, the Lily family's story is an old one," the reverend said. "Come with me, I'll show you."

I followed him to the parsonage. He opened the door using an enormous iron key. Something was bubbling in a pot on the stove. The smell of garlic and vegetable broth filled my nostrils as we walked toward the reverend's study. It was a small room with black wooden cupboards lining the walls. He opened one of the cupboards, closed it, opened the next one, closed that one, and then opened a third cupboard. After a brief search, he pulled out a heavy book.

"Here it is," he said. He laid the book on a table and carefully opened it. He fingered through the pages and stopped at a particular entry. "According to my records, the last of the Lily line, Reginald's son, Abton, left Applecross back in 1801. There have been no other entries since then."

"Is he the same Reginald who is buried in the Applecross cemetery?" I asked.

"Captain Reginald Lily, yes," the reverend said. "The one with the red ship. Or so the legend claims."

Just like the Eggstones house, I thought.

"A handsome man, so they said," the reverend continued. "And well liked in the village."

The Reverend told me how Reginald Lily's famous red ship had crashed into the coast in the first half of the eighteenth century. "I think that shipwreck was the most exciting event that happened in Applecross for several centuries!" he concluded with a hearty laugh.

I sighed. My dad had already told me the story about the red boat. I needed to know more than the simple tales the villagers told.

"What kind of people were the Lilys?" I asked. "I mean, what exactly were they doing in Applecross?"

"They were seen as benefactors," the reverend said.

"What kind of benefactors?" I asked.

"I think they were the kind of people who did a lot to help others," he said. "The type who were more interested in doing good deeds than receiving recognition or an award."

I smirked. "So they were wealthy?"

"I imagine so," the reverend said, grinning at my cynicism. "I'm probably not the most knowledgeable person on the subject, but I think they were traders."

"Traders?" I asked. "What did they trade?"

"I have no idea," the reverend said. "I know that they often took their ship out to sea so they could trade with the nearby islands."

That made me remember Aiby's comment about being able to spot the red house from the sea.

"Do you know anything about where they used to live?" I asked.

"Two centuries ago, they lived in the castle before it fell to ruin," the reverend said. "I believe they bought it from an aristocratic family."

I tilted my head. "They lived at the ruins?" I asked. "Really?"

"They were the last to ever reside there," the reverend said. "The castle has remained empty ever since Abton Lily, Reginald's son, left."

"Is it . . . haunted?" I asked.

The reverend boomed out a laugh. Normally I would have laughed at the idea, as well, but last night's events had me questioning everything. "Finley McPhee, please tell me you don't believe in ghosts at your age!"

I looked the reverend in the eyes. Just last night, I'd seen a blue flame that looked like a face floating atop Reginald Lily's grave. But I couldn't tell the reverend that. So I said nothing.

Reverend Prospero laid a heavy hand on my shoulder. "No one wanted to live at the castle because it was too big and too damp," he said. "That's all. And can you imagine how expensive it would be to heat all of those rooms in the winter? Believe me, its abandonment had nothing to do with ghosts!"

His answer didn't convince me, but I really couldn't argue with him, either. "Have you heard of a red house near Reginald Bay?" I asked.

The reverend pursed his lips. "A red house?" he said. "No, I can't say that I have." He narrowed his eyes at me. "Why all these questions about the Lily family, McPhee? What is it you really want to know?"

I could feel pins and needles in my hands. I knew I had to get out of there as quickly as I could. Thankfully, someone knocked loudly on the door. I walked over to answer it.

"McPhee, get back here!" the reverend shouted, pretending to be annoyed. "We haven't finished this discussion."

I put on my best fake smile. "I have to get back to work, Reverend," I said.

"Why are you taking such an interest in the Lily family?" he asked.

I put my hand on the door's handle. "I'm not taking

84

an interest in the Lily family," I said. "But I think they've come back to Applecross."

To make sure the reverend couldn't respond, I opened the door. Mr. Everett stood in the doorway. As always, he was carrying his little black book.

"Finley, wait a minute —" the reverend started, but I didn't answer. I was already out the door and on my way back to the post office.

Chapter
NINE

A SECOND LETTER,
LOST MEMORIES,
& AIBY'S FATHER

When I arrived at the post office, I found Patches diligently guarding my mailbag. Inside the bag, I found another letter addressed to the Lily family. This time the envelope was wrapped in brown packing paper, and the lettering of the address was red and jagged. It seemed to be etched into the envelope rather than simply written on it. No sender was listed, but the destination was clearly written:

The Lily Heirs
Enchanted Emporium
36 Eggstones Heaven
Reginald Bay, Applecross (Scotland)

This envelope referenced the Enchanted Emporium, which I'd completely forgotten to ask Aiby and the Reverend about. In fact, the only useful information I'd found so far was that the Lily family had been traders of some kind.

I grabbed my mailbag, jumped on Jules's bike, and sped around for the next few hours, delivering the mail.

By noon, Patches and I had made it to Burnt Beach. The surroundings seemed so different this time that I wondered if I was even on the same path. The strange sign with the crooked arrow was still there, but the rocks and blackened trunks from the day before were gone. In their place was a flourishing shrubbery and a few young trees. Green grass blanketed the ground and only the larger standing rocks were still visible. The rest of the barren landscape was gone.

"Patches, does anything seem strange to you?" I asked. He sniffed one of the young saplings, trotted around it, and then raised his leg over it. "I'll take that as a yes."

Feeling a little overwhelmed, I climbed off the bicycle and pushed it along the path. Apart from the new growth and vegetation, everything else seemed to be the same as before.

"Good morning," I said to a cranky-looking seagull.

For some reason, I knew that it was the same seagull I'd seen the day before. Patches barked at it once, then kept walking behind me.

This time I went right up to the red house. "I bet it was built from the wood of Captain Reginald's red ship," I said to myself, eyeing it with renewed curiosity.

The front door was wide open. "Aiby!" I called without thinking. "Stay here," I said to Patches. He sat on his hind legs.

"Aiby Lily?" I called. "I have another letter for you!"

No one answered. I noticed that the window beside the door looked more like a shop's window than a house's. Its wooden shutters were open. Inside, several shelves were crammed full of antique objects that looked like toys.

I tried to enter the house, but stopped. Well, I didn't stop — it felt like I was physically unable to step inside. As I stood in the doorway, I saw Aiby reading a large book and leaning against a curved counter. There was a huge flame-red rug beneath her feet. A wrought iron chandelier with dripping candles was suspended above her head. Behind her were dozens of shelves crammed with the most unusual collection of objects you could ever imagine.

I couldn't really distinguish anything specific because

it seemed like I was looking through a shifting mist. Shapes were fuzzy, colors were muted, and the shadows were dense.

"Aiby?" I called, still standing in the doorway.

She looked at me and it felt like magic. Her eyes seemed to pierce the blanket of mist that muddled my vision. The expression on her face was anxious.

I smiled awkwardly, and then mumbled something. I don't remember what I said or what happened afterward. As soon as the strange mist faded, I found myself walking by her side along the path in the woods. Patches was trotting a few paces in front of us as I guided Jules's bike over the stones on the ground.

Aiby was talking to me. I had the sensation of hearing everything but not understanding anything. I felt like a chunk of my life had vanished — first I had been talking to Aiby in the red house, and then the two of us were walking through the woods. *How did we get here?* I wondered.

At the time, I could never have understood because I didn't even know that Professional Memory Removal Dust existed. Aiby had dusted me with a magical powder to make me forget what I had seen. According to her, she'd done it for my own good, but I had my doubts.

Either way, all I felt was a vague sense of lost time. I

stopped abruptly in the middle of the forest path. "Isn't this a little weird?" I asked.

Aiby did a half-pirouette to face me. "What's weird?" she asked.

I pointed to the woods around us. "Just look around!" I said. "There are bushes, saplings, and grass! Yesterday there was nothing here but charred tree trunks."

She looked at me like I was talking about a flying rhinoceros, or something equally unlikely and strange.

I kneeled down to snap a twig off to make sure it was real. "See? They're real!"

"Of course they're real," Aiby said. "Don't you like them?"

"That's not the point!" I said.

"Then what is the point?" she asked.

"Come on, Aiby," I said. "Trees like this can't grow overnight."

"Well, it did rain last night," she said.

"It rains all the time!" I cried. "We're in Scotland!"

She crossed her long arms behind her back. I noticed she was wearing her usual mishmash of patterned clothing. Seeing her in the woods right then made her look like some kind of fairy creature.

Aiby rolled her eyes. "Dad planted them," she said. "He's really good at growing things."

"Growing trees overnight?" I said. "Yeah, right."

"They're for the official opening," she said, ignoring my sarcasm. "It didn't seem right for our first visitors to see this landscape of burned tree trunks."

I let out an exasperated sigh. "Aiby, what in the world are you even talking about?!"

"The opening of our store, Finley," she said. "Why else do you think the Lily family moved back to Applecross?"

"I had been wondering that," I said. "I even asked around in the village, but no one seemed to know anything about it."

"Really?" she asked.

Aiby was calm as could be, but I could feel the tension in me rising. Every response she'd given me seemed careful and prepared.

"Yes, I did," I said.

"And what did you discover, detective?" she asked.

"You're acting weird," I said.

"Think what you like," she said with a smile. "But I didn't spend the night searching for information on your family and their sheep farm."

"How did you know we have a sheep farm?" I asked.

Aiby picked a curl of wool from my clothes and lifted it up to my face.

"Oh," I muttered. "I guess everyone has a sheep farm in this area, anyway." I concentrated on pushing the bike. "I don't want you to think that I'm sticking my nose into your business or anything like that, but let's just say that I've noticed some strange things happening in the last few days."

Aiby shrugged. I didn't know what I wanted to say next, so I changed the subject. "What's the Enchanted Emporium?"

We had reached the sign that indicated the beginning of the path. "And while you're at it," I added, "can you explain to me why this arrow keeps changing positions?"

Aiby smiled at me. "Finley, are you sure you want to know?" she asked.

I was about to answer when I remembered her warning from the previous day. "No one can know everything," I said.

She nodded. "You were paying attention!" she said coyly. "I'll answer one of your two questions. Which one will it be?"

"The Enchanted Emporium," I said immediately.

"The store has always been our family's primary business," Aiby said proudly. "When it's our turn to run the shop, we open it for business."

"Your turn?" I asked. "What do you mean?"

"There are other families who share the business," Aiby explained.

"What *is* the business?" I asked.

"Selling, buying, and repairing rare items," she said.

"What kind of rare items?"

"Oh, I suppose things like the messages in bottles that you sometimes find on the beach," she said, smiling.

I narrowed my eyes at Aiby. I couldn't tell if she was trying to hint that she knew I'd found the bottle yesterday, or if she just brought it up because we'd talked about messages in bottles before.

I slumped my shoulders. "Listen, Aiby," I said. "I'm really confused."

"What is there to be confused about?" she asked.

I was about to say that her answer bothered me, but just then Patches began to run around our legs and bark. Someone was coming.

"There he is," Aiby said, using her hand to shade her eyes. "My father's finally home. Let's hope he's found who he was looking for in the village, otherwise we won't be able to open the shop on time."

That was when I recognized her father: he was the blond man with the self-propelling pants I'd followed to the cemetery the night before!

PROFESSIONAL
MEMORY
REMOVAL
DUST

The first documented use of **PROFESSIONAL MEMORY REMOVAL DUST** dates back to the nineteenth century when it was accidentally blown into the nostrils of the great Mexican musician, Marcel Castellano, in the middle of a performance. The dust made Marcello replay the first half of the composition all over again, inciting insults from the crowd — and a bullet from one critic's pistol.

Chapter
TEN

THE PROFESSOR,
A LIST OF NAMES,
& A FUNERAL

L ater that day, I was feeling flustered, so I went into town to try to clear my head.

"Finley, could you come here a moment?" Mr. Everett said. As usual, he was sitting on a wicker stool just outside the entrance to his shop and smoking his long pipe.

Mr. Everett's shop, The Curious Traveler, sold souvenirs and inexpensive gift items. From his stool, Mr. Everett was able to keep an eye on almost everything that happened in the main square of the village. Before retiring to Applecross, he had been a well-known professor at an important university. For this reason, some people in Applecross called him "The Professor." Mr. Everett didn't seem to mind.

I approached his shop. "Yes, Mr. Everett?" I asked.

"Can I have a word with you?" he asked. He glanced around quickly, then added in a whisper, "In private."

"Sure," I said.

He put his hands on his knees and raised himself up. He smoothed out the wrinkles in his blue business suit. "Please step inside," he said.

As I entered, the scent of lavender filled my nose. The shop was clean and organized, just like its owner. There were books, figurines, Scottish flags, scarves decorated with the colors of local rugby teams, wooden troll statues, and little elves holding twinkling glass gems in their hands.

Mr. Everett leaned across the pale wooden counter and looked me right in the eyes. "I've heard from the reverend that you've met the Lily family," he said.

Mr. Everett was usually direct, but it still caught me off guard. "Sort of," I mumbled. "Actually, I only asked the reverend if he knew anything about them."

"So why were you asking about them?" he asked.

I shrugged. Patches was scratching against the door outside the shop. "No particular reason," I answered.

Mr. Everett nodded thoughtfully. "Anyway, you were right," he said. "The Lily family has in fact returned to Applecross. Do you know why they've come back?"

I hesitated, uncertain how much information — if any — I should share with Mr. Everett. "They own a little shop," I said. "Down by the shore. It's called the Enchanted Emporium."

The Professor nervously traced his fingers along the wooden counter. I wondered if he was afraid that the opening of the new store would take away some of his business. "I must admit, I'm a little worried," he said. "I ran into Mr. Lily the other day when he came into the shop. He seemed pretty strange to me. I don't know why a man like him would want to open a shop in Applecross."

It's pretty strange for a former college professor to retire to Applecross to open a souvenir shop, too, I thought. But on the other hand, Mr. Everett was right — Mr. Lily was the strangest man I'd ever met.

"Have you spoken to him?" Mr. Everett asked. "Mr. Lily, I mean?"

I nodded. "We met briefly," I said.

"What about the girl?" he asked.

"We talked a little," I said. "She seems nice enough."

"I see," Mr. Everett said. He hesitated for a moment, then added, "Did they say if they were looking for someone in the village?"

"Looking for someone?" I repeated. It was true that

Aiby had talked about needing someone for the official opening, but I didn't know more than that.

A loud crash came from the shop's storage room. Mr. Everett spun with surprising speed. "Excuse me for one moment," he said. Then he disappeared into the storeroom. After a few moments of silence, I heard him rummaging around.

While I was alone in the shop, I took the opportunity to look around. I noticed a list of names by the cash register. The first name on the list was Askell. The second name was circled in red marker: Lily.

When Mr. Everett returned, I managed to turn my head around in time so that he wouldn't think I'd been looking at the list. "Pesky stray cats," he grumbled. "You only need to leave the door open a crack and they somehow manage to squeeze inside."

I had no reason to be suspicious of Mr. Everett. He was nice enough, and he certainly cared about Applecross. I figured he was probably just concerned about the future of his shop, so I decided to help him out without giving too much information away.

"Now I think about it," I said, "they did talk to me about some kind of grand opening in a week or so."

"I heard that as well," The Professor replied, nodding over at the McStay Inn on the other side of the square.

"Rufus McStay told me yesterday. There's a foreign man staying at his inn for the Enchanted Emporium's opening. In fact, Rufus asked me to go over and help interpret for his guest since the man refuses to come out of his room and only speaks Dutch."

"Maybe he's a friend of the Lily family," I said.

"In all likelihood, yes," Mr. Everett said. "Anyway, if you see the Lily family again, just be careful."

That sounded like a warning. "Mr. Everett, what do you really think about the Lily family?" I asked.

The old professor shook his head slowly. "Nothing," he said. "Their ancestors left a positive impression on the village, but that was over two hundred years ago. Time tends to change things."

"What do you mean?" I asked.

"Don't mind me, Finley," he said, flashing a smile. "I'm just being old and foolish."

I could tell that Mr. Everett wouldn't give me more information, so I turned to leave.

"Be careful, okay?" Mr. Everett repeated.

"I will," I said, wondering what he wasn't telling me.

As I opened the door, I nearly ran into Meb McCameron, the village dressmaker. She was holding a dark suit in her hands.

"Hi there, Finley," she said with her usual smile. She

turned to face Mr. Everett. "I've brought you your suit for the funeral."

Funeral? I thought, as the door closed behind me. *Who died?*

★ ★ ★

Mr. Everett's final warning of "Be careful" kept repeating in my head as I pedaled along my mail route. It was my last day delivering mail since Jules would be returning to work the following day. Halfway through my route, I decided to take a break and visit the ruined castle.

"Listen, Patches," I whispered. "How about the two of us go nose around the old Lily castle for a while?"

Patches howled softly. He didn't seem too happy about the idea of exploring a haunted castle, but I knew how to persuade him: I gave him one of his favorite treats. As he chewed, I slipped him into my mailbag and continued biking. I could feel him squirming the whole way.

It was such a clear day that I could see old lady Cumai on the other side of the bay. She was silhouetted against the calm sea, walking from the door of the flour mill to the cliff's edge.

The wind kept blowing my hair in my eyes and scattering my thoughts as I rode. Pedaling was twice

as hard as normal since the gusts of wind were strong enough to knock me off balance. I stopped for a rest, turning to look at the ruined castle up ahead. It looked like a rotten tooth poking out of the greenery.

Until I'd met Aiby, I only knew the castle as a setting for silly ghost stories. In the evenings, you could sometimes see car headlights moving around in the ruins. People often visited there at night if they wanted to feel the thrill of exploring a haunted house. Doug had told me not to go down there if I saw car headlights, but he'd never told me why. I only knew it was a place I never wanted to visit.

But things were different now. It felt as though those ruined walls were calling my name, as if the answers to the many questions I had about Aiby and her family could be found inside.

Earlier that day, when Aiby had introduced me to her father, we didn't really speak much. He didn't even shake my hand — he just waved at me and smiled briefly. I noticed he had the stubble-covered face of a man who was too busy to shave regularly. Or too lazy. But what really caught my eye was a strange-looking key that hung around his neck. On its stem was the engraving of a scarab beetle — just like the ones from ancient Egyptian hieroglyphics. It made me feel uneasy.

I pedaled a little faster. To reach the ruins, you had to cross over the small bridge that passed over Calghorn Dinn. Then you followed a dirt road that had mostly eroded over the years. There were countless potholes to avoid along the way, but eventually it would take you to the rear of the castle.

After I crossed the bridge, I had to pull off to the side of the road to let two cars pass me. It was unusual to see a single car on these roads, let alone two. The second car tapped the horn at me. I couldn't see who it was, but I lifted my hand and waved anyway.

Moving ahead, I noticed that the two cars were heading toward the Dogberry farm. There was something going on up there — the dogs were barking like mad, and there were three additional cars parked nearby.

I noticed the undertaker's car was already there. A broken-down car was next to the undertaker's. "Looks like bad news, Patches," I murmured. I jumped off the bike and observed the group of people on the farm. Moments later, I heard Reverend Prospero's booming voice.

That's what Meb was talking about with Mr. Everett, I realized. *Mr. Dogberry must have died.* "Poor man," I said. I hid the bike in some undergrowth by the side of the rode, and then I let Patches out from my bag.

It was sad news, but the two of us continued on our way toward the castle, anyway. People dying in Applecross wasn't all that unusual, after all. Doug claimed that dead people had gray skin, but I didn't know if that was true, because I'd never seen a dead person. In fact, I'd only seen a casket once, and it was closed.

Insects swarmed me as I passed through the woods. Branches whipped my face as I walked. Between one mosquito bite and the next, I wondered if I should have said a prayer for Mr. Dogberry. But if so, which one? I ran through a few in my head, but none of them seemed quite right. After all, I didn't even know how he had died.

Yet.

Chapter
ELEVEN

SNEAKING,
SHIVERING WORDS,
& A STRANGE STICK

"Heel, Patches," I whispered from the bushes. When I'd previously come to the ruins with Doug, we'd arrived by tractor from the front. Now that I was approaching the castle from the woods, it appeared larger and more imposing.

Patches and I approached the remains of an exterior wall. The large archway was nearly covered with countless tangles of creeping ivy. Inside the wall, wild grass was growing where the wood flooring used to be. It was a gray, gloomy, and empty space with a wooden roof that was falling to pieces. Above the archway, a wrought iron talon creaked softly in the wind. Once upon a time it had probably held a coat of arms or maybe a sign of some kind. I was more than a little creeped out

by the moaning sound it made when the wind hit it. It reminded me of the sounds a really sick person makes.

I noticed that the insects from the woods were keeping away from ruins. "No insects or spider webs nearby," I said to myself. "That's weird."

Patches wagged his tail, which helped me gather some courage. I pushed the curtain of creeping ivy aside and passed through the archway. "Let's go, Patches."

I wasn't looking for anything in particular, yet I felt I was heading in the right direction. After I passed through the first room, I entered a second archway and found myself outside again in a courtyard overrun by brambles. On one side, there were mounds of bricks that had once been the foundations of a building. Beyond that, there was a pathway that probably headed back to the dirt road. On the other side were the remains of a two-story house, half of which had collapsed in on itself. The roof beams protruded like stumps, which reminded me of a dead rabbit's ribcage being pulled apart to make rabbit stew.

I noticed some writing on the remaining plasterwork. It was mostly graffiti, like the names of people, hearts, and symbols — the usual things that kids write whenever they find somewhere private to hang out. The windows on the ground floor had been removed, and the ones on

the upper floor had been boarded up with pieces of spare wood. It was a depressing sight.

I cautiously approached the only open doorway. Patches followed warily. Only the hinges remained in the doorway. A low row of ferns brushed against my knees as I entered.

It was extremely cold inside the castle. It may sound weird, but it felt like the chill came from deep within me. Light filtered through cracks in the walls and the broken-down roof, but it was a cold light that didn't warm the skin.

I recognized the remains of a stone sink. There were hooks hanging from a wall that looked like they'd once held pots and pans. "This must be the kitchen," I said.

I carefully waded through the fern leaves and headed into a narrow wooden hallway. The floor creaked with every step. I involuntarily pictured myself falling through the floor into a basement filled with skeletons, chains, and rats. The thought made me silently curse all those horror films I'd watched on late-night TV.

Monsters or not, I didn't want to end up with a broken leg in a remote underground cellar. So I took my time.

"It's just an old abandoned house," I said to myself. "Quit acting like a baby, Finley."

What am I even doing here? I thought. The only justification I could come up with was that going to Aiby with my questions would probably just result in getting no answers — and more questions.

I looked around for Patches and saw his tail wagging among the ferns like a submarine's periscope. I whistled to him, and he was by my side in an instant. He trusted me as much as I trusted him — that fact alone gave me the courage to continue exploring.

The next room I entered had to have been the living room. A tree had grown in one corner and torn a hole through the ceiling. Huge bushes of wild berries completely covered another corner. The walls had tattered sections of wallpaper that were rotten and dry. I tore a strip off and it laid in my hand like a dead leaf. The pattern had diamond shapes with bees, scorpions, crickets, and scarab beetles inside them.

I thought back again to the key hanging around Aiby's father's neck. I decided that this was enough proof that the house had once belonged to the Lily family. "Look, Patches," I said. He stuck out his tongue and wagged his tail, obviously satisfied with my discovery.

A large stone chimney dominated the longest wall of the room. When I got up close to it, I discovered that someone had recently used the fireplace. Some

particularly brave kids from the village had probably started a fire there.

My father once told me that the castle had long ago been used by the village boys as the setting for some kind of initiation or rite of passage. To prove to the others that you were a man, you had to go into the castle and carry out a certain task, like stealing an object and bringing it back, opening one of the upstairs windows, or even spending a night inside the ruins. My friends hadn't continued these acts, although I sometimes wondered if Doug and his friends had.

Whoever had lit the fire seemed to have also scrawled a strange drawing on the chimney with a piece of coal. It looked like some kind of flaming pyramid. It reminded me of something I'd seen in my friend Jack's record collection. He had a bunch of 70s vinyl records that his dad had given to him. Since I didn't have anything to write on, I tried to memorize the drawing so I could ask Jack about it later.

I bent down to examine the fireplace. Upon closer inspection, I realized I had no way to really tell if a fire had been lit there two days ago, or two years ago.

While I was thinking about it, I heard what sounded like footsteps on the floor above me. Patches dashed into the next room like a stray bullet. "Patches!" I yelled.

I quickly jumped to my feet to follow him and smashed the back of my head against the chimney. My heart pounded in my chest and I felt dizzy.

"Dang it, Patches!" I said. "Get over here!"

Patches barked loudly. I rubbed my head and staggered after my dog until I entered a third room that was even darker and colder than the previous one. Patches was sitting at the bottom of a set of stairs. He had his paw on the first step, but he couldn't seem to find the courage to climb up. His sharp barking filled the house with a deafening echo.

The familiar tangle of creeping ivy and crumbling architecture surrounded us. The stairs were little more than wooden slats with large gaps missing from most of the steps.

I went up to Patches and I kneeled next to him. When I touched his fur, he jumped as though I'd given him an electric shock.

"Stop freaking out! There's no one up there," I said, although I was far from convinced. "It's probably just an animal of some kind. Maybe a badger, or a dormouse. Dad always says that once a dormouse gets into your house, they're impossible to get out!"

I tried to pull Patches away from the staircase, but he started to growl. Gradually, I was able to calm

him down. With silence surrounding us once again, it seemed worse than when Patches had been barking. The wooden beams creaked in the wind, and every nook and cranny seemed to sigh.

"It's only an animal, Patches," I said. "I mean, what else would be there?"

I stood on the first step and looked up the wooden staircase. The blowing wind created a strange noise that sounded like tinkling pieces of glass striking each other.

I was about to go up a second step but stopped when I saw something weird: there were thousands of letters written on the ceiling and walls in an unknown language. There were also a bunch of strange, creepy drawings made up of circles, pyramids, arrows, tridents, and other shapes.

I couldn't read a single letter of the bizarre writing. As I stared, the letters seemed to quiver as though there were tiny worms trapped underneath the plasterwork. It was like the walls were alive.

I rubbed my eyes, figuring it was a trick of the mind, but then the letters started changing shape. Very slowly, the writing began to resemble something readable.

"This is crazy," I whispered.

While the shifting letters reorganized themselves in front of my eyes, I saw something else at the top of the

stairs: a fragment of a broken mirror. It was reflecting the outline of a man who was on the top floor. Again I heard footsteps above me — and this time I was sure I hadn't imagined them.

I picked up Patches. "Let's go!" I said.

As I ran, the Lily house seemed to shrink and expand like it was breathing. The walls of the drawing room groaned like the bowels of a sinking submarine. As I carried Patches through the kitchen, I heard a deep wail coming from the water pipes. I ran faster.

When we finally got outside, I tripped over the brambles. Patches and I went flying. I landed on my chest and lay still for a moment, collecting my thoughts. Then I heard a bang from the direction of the roof. I jumped to my feet and saw a flock of blackbirds take flight from the rooftops.

"Let's go!" I yelled a second time, then started running again. I ignored the pain in my chest and continued to pump my legs. I checked back once to make sure Patches was following me and saw that he was just a few paces behind. We ran through the archway, through the creeping ivy, and half slid, half ran down the path through the woods. I dodged tree branches faster than I thought I could even move. The adrenaline made my ears hum.

I finally stopped running when I saw Jules's bike glimmering under the brush. I rested my hands on my knees and drew in huge, gasping breaths. Little by little, the sheer terror I felt transformed into nervous giggling. Moments later, I was rolling around on the ground and laughing like a madman.

I climbed back to my knees and scratched Patches behind the ears. *Back to the land of the living,* I thought with another chuckle.

"What happened in there?" I said to Patches, still breathing hard.

I moved aside the last of the bushes covering the bike, unable to shake the horrible feeling I'd gotten inside the ruined castle. It was like the house had come to life, a beating heart and lungs and all. Safe by the road and warm in the sun, I found it much easier to explain away the experience as simply a product of my overactive imagination.

"I just imagined it all," I told myself. "Even still, I'm never going back to that house again."

I walked the bike out from the brush and onto the road — then I saw her and froze. "Aiby?" I asked in amazement. "What are you doing here?"

Aiby Lily was about ten feet ahead with her back to me. She was barefoot and wearing a dress with green,

red, and purple stripes that went to a few inches above her knees.

Patches dashed off toward Aiby, wagging his tail in excitement. "Finley!" she cried. "Where have you been?!"

"What do you mean?" I asked, completely confused.

Aiby held a long, curved stick in her hand that was almost as tall as she was. "I don't have time to explain!" she said, motioning with the stick. "Give me your hand!"

I could see that she was frightened — maybe even more frightened than I was. So I reached out for her.

Aiby rapped the stick on the ground and said: "Home!" In an instant, we found ourselves in front of the red house in Reginald Bay.

THE TRIP STICK

The **Trip Stick** is a magical object fashioned from the trunk of an inter-dimensional maple tree. The stick can store eleven locations in its memory by leaving Journey Signs at specific locations, allowing the stick's user to instantly teleport to any of them. Teleportation is activated by beating the stick on the ground and saying the name of the place to which you wish to travel.

ENCHANTED EMPORIUM

Chapter
TWELVE

SECRETS,
HOMICIDAL SWORDS,
& MR. LILY

y jaw dropped open in disbelief, but Aiby didn't give me time to ask any questions. "This way!" she said. "Quickly!"

Aiby dragged me to the side of the red house that overlooked the sea. I saw her father — he was backed into a corner between the house and the edge of a cliff. His hands were raised like a fighter's, and his face was bloodied and terrified.

"At last!" Mr. Lily yelled when he saw us appear.

I couldn't believe my eyes — a floating sword was dancing around in front of Mr. Lily! Its tip was aimed at him as it rotated menacingly in midair. It had a long, flat blade with a vicious-looking, jagged edge. Its iron hilt had a large, strange-looking stone set into it.

It was clear that Mr. Lily was trapped. If he moved to the side, the sword would be able to strike his body. If he moved forward, the sword would pin him farther back into the corner.

"What the heck is going on?!" I asked Aiby.

"It's all my fault!" she said. "I freed it by accident!"

"You freed it?" I asked.

"It's a Djinni Wizard Slayer from the thirteenth century," Aiby explained. "It fell out of its sheath when I was polishing it and immediately attacked father. It's a miracle that he's still alive."

Mr. Lily dodged a frontal thrust. "Not for much longer," he cried. "Unless you do something — and fast!"

I blinked hard. "Wizard Slayer?" I repeated.

"It's a magical sword," Aiby said, clearly getting agitated.

"So your father is a wizard?" I asked.

"Do you mind if we answer your questions later?" Mr. Lily yelled.

Aiby tried to pull me forward, but I didn't budge. "He's not a wizard," she said, "and neither am I, but that sword is magical. And the only way to stop it is for a man to grab hold of it."

I pointed at myself, dumbfounded. "You mean me?" I asked. "But I'm not even in high school yet!"

"You're the only male I know here," she said, pleading with me. "I'd do it myself if I could!"

The sword cut through the air and missed Mr. Lily's leg by less than an inch. "Ah!" he shouted. "Stop bickering with each other and help me!"

"Finley!" Aiby cried. "You're our only hope of stopping it. There's no other way according to what's written in the BBMO."

"What the heck is the BBMO?" I asked.

"*The Big Book of Magical Objects*," she said. "Do you remember what I was reading the other day when you came to the shop?"

I tried, but the memory was all hazy. I shook my head.

Aiby slapped her forehead. "Of course you can't!" she said. "I had to use the Professional Memory Remover Dust on you."

Now I was completely lost. "Huh?" I said.

Mr. Lily yelled out. "For Djinni's sake, boy! Just do what my daughter tells you! Now!"

Aiby gave me a gentle push forward, putting me less than four steps away from the magical sword. "I don't understand what's going on here, Mr. Lily!" I cried. "The other night I saw you on the road with a bunch of flowers. And then — and then you . . ."

The sword darted forward. "I know, boy! I know!" Mr. Lily said. "I know it all seems strange to you right now, but I assure you there's an explanation. But if you don't mind, I'd rather not be turned into a shish kebab."

I took a slow step toward the sword, worried that it might turn on me at any moment. "But what about your pants, Mr. Lily?" I whispered. "They were walking!"

"Yes, yes, they're my special pants!" Mr. Lily cried. He was now at the edge of the corner on the cliff. "And before you ask, I then used a very ordinary flask of Spirit Powder and some other basic relics from the mid-eighteenth century. Now can you please do something about this Wizard Slayer?"

I took another step forward. The sword was now within my reach. It shimmered menacingly in the air.

"I just have to grab it?" I asked.

"Just take it by the handle," Aiby said. "It won't hurt you, it only cares about my father!"

Then why are you standing so far away from me? I thought.

"It's moving so fast," I said. I could barely keep up with the movement of the sword while trying to ignore my maddeningly rapid heartbeat.

"Have courage, Finley!" Aiby whispered. She had moved closer now. I could smell her perfume on the air.

The sword, the sword, I repeated in my head. *Take hold of the sword. Just grab it!*

I closed my eyes. I just couldn't do it.

Then I heard Aiby's voice. "The other day, when you were about to enter the shop, Finley," she said, "I asked you something."

My heart skipped a beat. I opened my eyes again. The sword was dangling close to where my hands were. I could feel the subtle shifts of air it was creating.

"I asked you if you were afraid of me," Aiby said. "Do you remember what you said?"

I shook my head, but kept my eyes focused on the hilt of the sword. "No, I don't remember."

"You said you weren't afraid of me," Aiby said. "That's the reason I came to get you. I need someone who isn't afraid. Not of me, or that sword!"

I smiled. A moment later, my fingers closed around the grip and squeezed hard. I could feel the cold metal in my palm. At first it was like holding a metal snake, or pulling in a tug-of-war in the midsummer Highland games. A second later, the blade went still and the tip fell to the ground.

"Don't let go of it!" Mr. Lily shouted, running toward me. He yanked the sword from my hands and pushed me out of the way. I fell to the ground in a heap.

Without saying another word, Mr. Lily stomped toward the red house. I heard him swearing under his breath at Aiby's carelessness, my hesitation, and the Djinni Wizard Slayer itself. A moment later, Mr. Lily slammed the door shut and I couldn't hear him anymore.

Aiby sat down next to me. "Sorry, Finley," she said. "He's really angry, but he didn't mean to hurt you. I'm so grateful for what you did for him."

I brushed the dirt off my shirt. "You know what, Aiby?" I said. "I think we need to have a nice, long talk."

She anxiously glanced back at the red house. "Not here," she said, "and not now."

As far as I knew, a screaming axe or a singing lance could emerge from the house at any moment, so another time and place was just fine by me. "Tomorrow, then," I said calmly. "Should I come to pick you up, or will you just . . . teleport there?"

Aiby smiled, apparently amused by my joke. She was still holding the stick that had teleported us here. "It can only bring me to places where I've left a Journey Sign," she explained.

I had no idea what she was talking about. Frankly, between my escape from the castle and the homicidal sword, I'd had enough excitement and mystery for one day.

We agreed to meet at the flour mill at three in the afternoon the next day. "And no games this time," I said. "Promise me you won't use memory erasing gadgets or any other stupid stuff like that."

Aiby nodded. "Okay," she said. "I promise."

"And no more lies," I added. "If you want me to trust you, then you have to trust me."

"I never lied to you," she muttered.

"Telling me the truth and then forcing me to forget it isn't any different than lying," I said.

Aiby blushed. Or maybe it was just a reflection of light from the red walls of the Enchanted Emporium. I noticed for the first time that there was a ladder by the entrance of the house where they were hanging a shop sign.

I said goodbye, and Aiby ran back toward the house.

"One last thing," I shouted before she disappeared inside.

Aiby stopped on the doorstep and turned to face me.

"That stuff about courage," I said. "You said that I said I wasn't afraid of you. Did I really say that?"

Aiby frowned at me, fixing her green eyes on mine. She didn't speak.

I sighed. "Okay, then," I said. "I'll ask you tomorrow."

Chapter
THIRTEEN

DOUBTS,
DEMANDS,
& ANSWERS

My bedroom looked like a cop's office from a TV crime show. All the information I had about the Lily family was pinned to the wall. I thought that seeing it all laid out might help me figure out the mysteries from the last few days.

On one side of a sheet of paper, I wrote "Lily" and tacked it to the wall with a pin. Underneath that, I tacked several more pieces of paper. On each piece of paper, I wrote things I'd seen over the last few days that involved the Lily family in some way. The words were: *spider, bicycle, Wizard Slayer, Spirit Powder, talking dead, Self-Propelling Pants, Trip Stick, Memory Remover Dust,* and *the BBMO* (The Big Book of Magical Objects).

To the right of those words, I tacked the word *Unexplained*. Beneath that heading, I hung pieces of paper with the following words written on them: *store opening, fast-growing trees on the promontory, talking seagull, the ancient castle, Mr. Everett's list of names, the Dutch guest at the McStay Inn,* and *riddle in the bottle.*

At the very bottom, I wrote out the riddle from the message in the bottle. Looking at all those words written out, it seemed strange to think that only a week before, I'd been complaining that my life in Applecross was boring.

As I stared at the wall, I considered all this strange information and looked for some sort of connection. I spent a long time thinking about that message in the bottle as I walked back and forth in my room. Still, nothing jumped out at me. Patches tried and failed to find a place to sit where he could keep an eye on me without getting stepped on.

Think, Finley, I thought. *Just think.*

I went over the riddle again in my mind. *Four men and one woman,* I thought. *They run, she doesn't. The men get wet, she doesn't.*

I tried to find a connection between the Self-Propelling Pants that belonged to Aiby's father and the riddle in the bottle, but that didn't seem to add up. I just

couldn't figure out what the rest of that story had to do with the color of their clothing.

So I went over the riddle again. And again. No luck.

When I'd stopped pacing, I could hear my parents downstairs discussing dinner and local news. It wasn't anything particularly exciting — one of the Corman sheep had escaped from its enclosure, and Mr. Dogberry had died in his sleep.

I threw myself onto my bed and buried my head under the pillow. Nothing made any sense. I decided to take a nap in the hopes that a fresh look at things might help me see something I'd missed.

But before I could even close my eyes, Doug burst into my room. "So, little brother," he said, leaning down until he was an inch from my nose. "Spit it out. Let's hear it."

I would have gladly told him what he wanted to know just to get him to leave, but I had no idea what he was talking about.

"Come on in, Doug," I said sarcastically.

My brother tilted his head and put a hand on my shoulder. It felt like it was made of rock — just like the rest of Doug.

"Stop kidding around," he said. "I know why you've been hiding in your room all day."

"Oh, yeah?" I said. I glanced over at the wall with my notes pinned to it. "You're getting brighter every day, brother."

Suddenly, Doug stood up from the bed. The rebounding springs in the mattress nearly tossed me onto the floor.

"Let me guess, then," he said. "Violet?"

I stared at him with a blank look on my face.

"Helena?" he added. "Or maybe Lauren?"

"Doug, what the heck are you talking about?" I asked.

He crossed his arms over his chest. "Come on, Finley," he said. "Just confess."

I sighed. "Okay," I said. "Let's see . . . I was absent seventy-one days from school this year, so they failed me. I stole your Victory of the High Seas fishing pole and hid it in a hollow trunk down by the stream. And yes, I'm the one who ate all three of the chocolate chip cookies that were in the kitchen. Anything else you want to know?"

In a heartbeat, Doug pinned me to the bed with his arms. I'd forgotten how quick he was despite his size. "You little brat!" he growled. "I knew you were the one who stole my fishing pole, but I don't care about that right now."

I could hardly breathe. "Get off me!" I cried. "I'm suffocating!" I tried to kick him off, but it was like moving the anchor of a fishing boat.

"I don't care if you suffocate, Viper," he said. "Either you tell me the name of the new girl in the village, or you're going to pass out."

He knows about Aiby, I realized. *How did he find out?*

My brother pushed me even deeper into the mattress. "I saw her at the supermarket," Doug said. "She was buying up a bunch of bandages and ice packs. Dad asked her if everything was okay, but she just nodded. I got a pretty good look at her, and boy is she cute. How old is she? Do you know? Fourteen? Sixteen? Did she tell you?"

I tried to speak, but Doug just rambled on. "I know you know," he said, smirking. "Guess how I know."

I opened my eyes wide and shrugged as best I could, hoping he would just tell me. "Because she knew who I was," Doug explained. "She said to me, 'You're Doug, aren't you?' And then she said, 'Finley told me all about you.'"

I tried to say that wasn't true, but only managed to squeeze out a few strangled syllables. I hadn't told her anything about Doug, my mother, or my father. At least, I couldn't remember telling her anything about them.

Doug shook me, giving me a chance to breathe.

"What did you tell her about me, little brother?" he asked. "Did you tell her that I was the best rugby player in the Highlands? That I've got a tryout with Glasgow Warriors in September? Did you tell her all that?"

He jerked me again with each question. I was understanding less and less about what was going on. I tried to speak, but couldn't.

Doug released his grip. "Say that again," he said, putting his ear to my mouth.

"Wilma," I muttered. "Her name is Wilma."

Doug's eyes lit up. "Yes," he murmured, letting go of me. "Wilma. It's a perfect name for her." He looked obscenely happily. "I should've guessed."

While Doug was strutting around the room, I sat on the bed and rubbed my aching neck. "You're an animal, Doug," I said. "You could have strangled me."

"Shut up, momma's boy," he said. He went over to my notes on the wall and looked them over. "What's all this junk, Viper?" I started to speak, but he cut me off. "Nevermind, I just realized I don't care." He laughed. "Mom says it's time for dinner."

Upon hearing the word *dinner*, Patches ran downstairs, his tail wagging happily. I staggered up from the bed, still aching and angry.

Doug was still looking at my note-covered wall. After a moment, he said, "She's dead."

My eyes went wide. "What?" I asked.

Doug pointed at the riddle written on the wall. "The lady in that riddle," he said. "She's dead."

I blinked. "What are you talking about?" I asked.

"It's so obvious, Viper!" Doug said. "Don't you get it? They're at a funeral! The woman's dead. The four men are the pallbearers carrying the casket. They start to run when it starts to rain, but she doesn't. You know, because she's dead. Doofus."

My jaw dropped. "So she doesn't get wet," I said, "because she's in the casket!"

Doug formed an imaginary pistol with his finger and pointed it at me. "And they say I'm the dumb one," he said with a smirk. Then he left my room.

I glanced at my wall. Doug may have solved the riddle, but now I was even more confused than before.

Chapter
FOURTEEN

QUESTIONS,
ANSWERS,
& MORE QUESTIONS

Aiby arrived at three in the afternoon the next day. We met on the road from the promontory and walked in silence, heading away from the flour mill toward the small lakes at Calghorn. We reached the oak tree where the skull and sign were, and then we took the path to the left. It brought us directly to my secret place by the stream. I motioned for her to sit down.

"So this is your secret place," she said.

"That's right," I said.

She smiled and sat next to a spring of crystal-clear water. "It's lovely here."

"Thank you," I said.

I wondered if she knew how beautiful she looked just then. She was wearing long, multi-colored pants and

a shirt that was made of patches with an asymmetrical hem. She had three different necklaces on, and her socks didn't match.

There was an obvious awkwardness between us, so we didn't say anything for a while. Only Patches seemed comfortable. He went back and forth between us so we'd take turns petting him.

Aiby realized I wasn't going to talk first. "Where do you want me to start?" she asked.

"Let's start with the flying sword," I said. Then I quickly added, "Oh, and how is your dad doing?"

"He has a few scratches, but nothing too serious," Aiby said. "His pride is wounded more than anything else."

I nodded. "It's not every day you get attacked by a flying sword," I said. "That is, if what I saw was even real."

"Listen, Finley," Aiby said. "I know I owe you some explanations."

"That's why we're here, isn't it?" I asked.

"Yes," Aiby said, "it is. But if my dad knew I was talking to you . . ."

"He won't hear it from me," I said.

Aiby nodded. "Okay," she said. "But I don't know where to start."

I wasn't sure what to ask, so I just listened to the sounds around me. I heard a soft rustle in some nearby bushes. The constant buzzing of insects filled the air. Water tumbled through some stones.

I decided I'd start with a simple question. "What are you?" I asked. "A fairy creature? An alien? Some sort of time traveler?"

Aiby smiled. "None of the above," she said, crossing her arms. "I told you that our family business, the Enchanted Emporium, trades in antique goods. That isn't the whole truth, though."

"I know," I said.

"The truth is," she said slowly, "we trade in magical items."

"Magical items," I echoed.

"That's right," Aiby said. "The Enchanted Emporium has always bought, sold, and repaired them along with their related accessories."

I raised an eyebrow at her. "Yeah, right."

"Magical items really do exist," Aiby insisted. "Today they're more like collectors' items, but they do exist! I know you've probably only read about them in fairy tales or fantasy fiction, but they're real."

"I don't read much, Aiby," I said. "So how do they work?"

"My father's magical pants, the dust that I sprinkled in your face to make you forget that you'd seen me in the shop, that little spider that I used to repair your bicycle, and the stick that we used to teleport — they are all magical items. They've been studied, researched, and cataloged in the *Big Book of Magical Objects*. My favorite items are the Seven-League Boots, the Ring of the Nibelung, and Sinbad the Sailor's Flying Carpet."

"And you sell them?" I asked.

Aiby laughed. "Obviously not all of them," she said. "There are far too many magical items to keep in one place, but we know about most of them. The BBMO describes them all. Well, the ones we know about, anyway."

"Kind of like the *Register of Cattle Breeds*?" I asked.

"Something like that, yes," Aiby said. "I know it seems ridiculous to you, but it's been our family's business for over a thousand years."

I whistled. "Then I imagine it's a profitable business."

"Not really," Aiby said. "You see, the truth is that a Lily ancestor of mine opened the first Enchanted Emporium back in 868 in China."

"Why China?" I asked.

"I don't know — you'd have to ask Dad," Aiby said. "What I do know is that it was a Lily who first came up with the idea of establishing a shop that sells magical objects. He had invented a magical book, the first ever to have moving letters, almost six hundred years before Gutenberg was born. As I understand it, my ancestor sold the book to the sovereign ruler of the Celestial Empire of China."

While Aiby talked, I tried not to look at her so it would be easier to concentrate on what she was saying. But even then, I was fascinated by the musical sound of her voice. I didn't want to interrupt her, so I didn't tell her that the book with moving letters reminded me of those shifting words that were on the walls inside the castle. So she just continued her story while I kept my eyes on the ground in front of me.

"What I'm telling you is a family secret," Aiby said. "My ancestor opened the first store. After his death, the store passed to his son, and —"

"Let me guess," I said. "From heir to heir and so on until your father became the lucky owner."

Aiby shook her head. "My dad didn't want the responsibility of owning the shop," she said. "He was worried about the trouble that comes with it. You see, magical objects attract all kinds of collectors, but not all of them are good. There are many dark souls who want the objects for selfish or sinister reasons."

I had already dreamed up a couple of ways to use the Memory Remover Dust at school, but I figured they'd all fall under selfish or slightly sinister. So I kept my mouth shut.

"My ancestor chose six different families as successors," Aiby said. "Then he drew up a system where these six families, and their descendants, would take turns managing the Enchanted Emporium. After six turns, the keys to the shop would return to the first family, and then the cycle would repeat."

"So that's why you returned to Applecross?" I said.

Aiby sighed. "Because it's our turn again, yes," she said.

"And Reginald was the last Lily family member to run it," I said.

Aiby nodded. "You've been paying attention," she said. She scooped up a handful of pebbles and began to toss them into the lake, one by one. "Dad and I left London to come here to find Reginald's house and open the shop."

"How did you know it was your turn?" I asked.

Aiby shrugged. She tossed another pebble into the water. "One day the keys just arrived at our doorstep," she said.

"The keys?" I asked.

Aiby showed me one of the necklaces that she was wearing around her neck. It was made of gold, and the stem was in the shape of a cricket. "This is one of the keys for the Enchanted Emporium that now belong to the Lily family," she said. "What would you think if you received a key like this?"

"That the mailman was nuts," I said. "Can I see it?"

Aiby handed it to me. The cricket, still hanging from Aiby's neck, was warm to the touch. While I turned it over in my hand, I couldn't focus on anything but the fact that we were only a few inches from each other.

"How many keys are there?" I asked quietly.

"Four," she said softly.

The key with the scarab beetle stem that had been hanging around her father's neck popped into my head. "So each one is different?" I asked.

"Yes," she said. "Mine is in the shape of a cricket, but there's also a scorpion, a bee, and a scarab beetle. Four insects. To open the Enchanted Emporium, you need four people."

"It must have a pretty complicated lock," I said.

Aiby smiled. "In a way," she said. She began to look for more pebbles.

"What's inside the red house?" I asked.

"Right now it's just a mess because we're still doing

the inventory," she said. "The shelves are mostly filled with magical books, ink, and things like that. The Lily family has always specialized in books."

"And that Wizard Slayer sword," I said.

"Actually, we have three of them," Aiby said. "Plus a King's Killer and a Corpse Crusher."

"Oh," I said, unable to imagine what those things might be.

Aiby grinned, seemingly reading my thoughts. "One was a legendary king's battle-axe," she said. "And the other bursts into flames in certain situations. We also have the label from a Cloak of Invisibility."

"What about the cloak itself?" I asked.

Aiby shrugged and laughed. "My dad can't seem to find it," she said with a smirk. "But he has managed to track down the miniature army of copper soldiers belonging to Ludwig of Bavaria, a dozen magical wands that still have to be cataloged, six magical glass eyes, two skeletons belonging to creatures that never existed, plus about a hundred boxes and packages and parcels of varying shapes and sizes." Her voice grew fainter as she talked. "As you can imagine, they're all very old items. Just giving an item a name is a long and complicated process." She paused for a moment. "Do you remember that day you appeared at the door?"

"A little," I said.

"Do you remember what you saw inside?" she asked.

"Everything was hazy," I said. "It was like a fog that clouded my vision."

"That's right," Aiby said. "Do you remember that you were physically unable to enter?"

"Yes," I said, remembering. "Was it a magical force field, or something?"

Aiby laughed. "No, not at all," she said. "It was because you weren't carrying a magical object with you. It's one of the three rules of the Emporium."

"What are the other two rules?"

"Everything is paid for in gold," Aiby said, "and payment must come up front."

I laughed. "So no credit," I said. Aiby nodded. The Enchanted Emporium didn't seem all that different from the village shops in that way. "Are you expecting a lot of customers?"

Aiby shrugged. "Does it matter?"

"I mean, are there lots of wizards around?" I asked.

"You don't need to be a wizard to buy or sell at the Emporium," Aiby said. "In fact, Dad says that wizards no longer exist, if they ever did at all. There are only collectors of magical items, or those who just need theirs repaired."

"Like what?" I asked. "Replacing a heel, or fixing a buckle?"

"Yeah, those kinds of things," she said. "Also, buying the various ingredients for spells, love potions, friendship powders — stuff like that."

I smirked. "What kind of ingredients?" I asked. "Bat bones, parrot tongues, Edelweiss petals collected under a full moon?"

Aiby rolled her eyes. "Kind of, yes," she said.

"And that's your job?"

Aiby shook her head. "No, I only sell the items," she said. "Dad is the one who searches for them in our family. It can be, um, dangerous."

"And the other two people?" I asked.

"We haven't found them yet," Aiby said.

That must be who they were searching for in the village, I thought.

"Why do you need them?" I asked.

"I don't know if I should say," Aiby muttered.

I shrugged and nodded. "If you can't tell me, then don't worry about it."

Aiby thought for a moment. "We're looking for someone who can protect the Emporium."

"From whom?" I asked.

A cloud passed in front of the sun. "There are dangers

that I can't tell you about," Aiby said. "You saw some of those things with your own eyes already. Thankfully, I found you in time."

Neither of us said anything for a long time. I knew there was a lot she still hadn't told me, but the little she had already said would be giving me nightmares for a while. It made me wonder what the people of Applecross would do when they learned that a magical store was opening in their village.

I figured I'd ask about something safer. "What's all this stuff about the six families?" I asked.

"There are seven families, actually," Aiby said. "They aren't the initial families who began everything, but there are always only seven. We are one family. There's also the Scarselli family, the Tiagos, the Askells —"

I held my hand up to stop her. "Wait, what was the last name you said?"

"The Askells," Aiby repeated. A long shiver ran down my spine.

"I've heard that name before," I said. "Well, that's not completely true. I've *read* that name before."

Aiby narrowed her eyes. "Where?"

"It was written down on a list in Mr. Everett's shop," I said.

Aiby just stared at me.

"Do you know who Mr. Everett is?" I asked.

Aiby shook her head. "Do you know who the Askells are?" she asked, her green eyes more intense than ever.

I got the sense that she was very interested in the Askells.

This incredible carpet, unlike its fictional
literary namesake, is completely genuine. It has
nine symbols woven into the fabric. When touched,
these symbols allow for in-flight navigation. During
flight, the user must simply shift their weight from
one symbol to another in order to speed up,
slow down, or turn the carpet.

Chapter
FIFTEEN

THE MCSTAY INN,
AN EMPTY SUITCASE,
& ROOM 19

At five o'clock that same afternoon, Aiby and I made our way through the main square of Applecross toward The Curious Traveler. I pedaled my bike while Aiby rode on the handlebars. After the ankle injury, the post office had given Jules a scooter. Now Jules sputtered around the country roads on his new ride, causing all the dogs to bark well before he arrived. He gave the bike to me as thanks for covering his route while he was laid up. That was just fine by me, since riding the bike was much faster than walking everywhere.

Earlier that day, Aiby had insisted on speaking to Mr. Everett to find out why he was interested in the Askell family and how he knew the name. As far as Aiby knew,

the names of the seven families who took turns running the Enchanted Emporium were only known to each other.

I slowly came to a stop in front of The Curious Traveler. Aiby gracefully hopped off the handlebars and walked toward the shop window. "It looks closed," she said.

I put a hand on the cushion of The Professor's favorite chair. It felt cold, meaning Mr. Everett hadn't been here for a while. I pushed against the door, but it was locked. Patches sniffed at the crack between the door and the step.

"Was this where you saw the list?" Aiby asked.

"Yeah," I said. "Behind the counter."

"Tell me again what Mr. Everett is like," Aiby said.

"He's a pretty quiet guy," I said. "He's a retiree and spends most of his time chatting with villagers and writing in a little black book that he always keeps with him. He's a former professor, he sings in the church choir, and his shop sells souvenirs." It wasn't much information, but it was everything I knew.

We went around to the back of the shop to an alleyway that led to Dusker's garage in one direction and a small fenced-off grassy area in the other. We didn't find Mr. Everett in either place.

I remembered that Mr. Everett complained about the cats that were sneaking into his back room whenever he left the door ajar.

"Hold on a second," I said. I made sure no one was watching, then I scurried up the fence. "I just want to check if the back door is open."

Patches leaned against the fence with his paws in a futile attempt to climb the fence along with me.

When I'd reached the door, Aiby asked, "Is it open?"

The handle didn't budge. "It's locked," I said.

As I was climbing back over the fence, I noticed something glittering in the grass nearby. I walked over to examine it, but it was just a shard of glass.

"Where else we can look for Mr. Everett?" Aiby asked.

An idea came to me. "Come with me," I said.

We crossed back over Applecross's main square and entered the McStay Inn. The rugs on the floors were packed with dust and the curtains reeked of cooking smells from the kitchen. The ceiling of the inn was so low that Aiby had to hunch a little to avoid hitting her head. The McStays had prohibited smoking twenty years ago, but the stale scent of tobacco still lingered in the air. Everything creaked, even the lights, and I swore I could hear cockroaches scurrying around inside the walls. I'd

heard many times that hot water hadn't passed through the pipes of the inn in years, meaning cold showers were mandatory.

I could go on, but I won't. Needless to say, the McStay Inn wasn't the most welcoming of places. However, many tourists still stayed there, claiming it had "character" due to its no-frills, no-nonsense form of Scottish hospitality.

We found Rufus McStay wedged between two couch cushions in the reception area. He sat in front of a wall with a stuffed owl and a bunch of keys hanging on it. I didn't see any guests.

"McPhee," Rufus said. His eyes slid to the side for a moment to see my companion, then came back to me. "How's your old man?"

He crushed my hand with a firm handshake. "My father is doing well, Mr. McStay," I said, doing a decent job of hiding the pain.

"What can I do for you?" he asked. He was watching Aiby while she examined the framed hunting photographs on the wall. I could see that Mr. McStay was curious about my friend, but I decided to ignore it.

"I'm looking for Mr. Everett," I said. "Is he here?"

"The Professor? Why?" Mr. McStay said in his booming voice.

"He mentioned a Dutch guest who was staying

here," I said, remembering that Mr. Everett said he'd been needed as a translator.

"Oh, yes, that scoundrel!" Rufus McStay said. "Our Dutch guest is crazy — completely crazy!"

At that point, Aiby turned around to look at Mr. McStay for the first time. "Do you like those photos?" he asked her. "They were taken in the summer of '76, the famous summer a thousand wild boars . . ."

Oh, no, I thought. *Not that story again.*

"Why is your Dutch guest crazy?" I asked, trying to distract him before he started one of his long and boring tales. But it was too late — with a new listener for his stories, Rufus McStay certainly wasn't going to stop now.

I sighed, realizing I would learn no more about the mysterious Dutchman. I tried to find a way to escape from Rufus McStay's story, but Aiby seemed perfectly relaxed. She smiled sweetly at Mr. McStay and allowed him to show her one photo, and then another. After a few moments of listening patiently, Aiby cleverly asked a question about Mr. Everett and the so-called crazy Dutchman.

"Thank goodness The Professor came to the rescue!" Mr. McStay said. "I didn't have a clue what that foreigner wanted. He was furious about something or other, and he refused to leave the inn for three whole days. As far

as I could tell, he wanted to know about the full moon. He's a complete lunatic, I tell you. This morning he disappeared at the crack of dawn without even leaving a note."

"Did he pay you at least?" Aiby asked.

Mr. McStay's chest puffed up. "I knew that fella was trouble as soon as I set eyes on him, so I made him pay for the whole week in advance."

"So he might come back?" Aiby asked.

"Who knows," Mr. McStay said. "The keys to room number nineteen are hanging right behind me. If he comes back, his bed is still available."

Just then, Aiby winked at me — and believe it or not, I knew exactly what she wanted me to do. She pointed at another hunting photo, feigning interest in it so that the innkeeper would turn his back to me.

I slipped behind the counter, ignoring the baleful look the stuffed owl seemed to be giving me, and snatched the key to room nineteen. As quiet as a mouse, I disappeared up the deteriorating wooden staircase, and then wandered through a narrow hallway.

I was trying to find room nineteen, but the inn's numbering system defied all logic. Room sixteen followed room two, and room nine was next to room twenty-one. Room five was in the attic — and right across from the

room I was looking for. I pulled the key from my pocket, slipped it into the lock, and turned. The door opened quietly.

As I stepped inside, I saw that the room was small. It looked like it had been crammed into the corner of the building. The roof's beams were exposed, and it had one low window that looked out over the church. A gap in the window's seal let in the chilly evening air, but the room still smelled stale. There was also a lingering smell of incense.

I felt uneasy. After all, I was searching through an unknown person's room while anyone could easily walk in on me. I didn't even know what I was looking for.

I noticed the bed was unmade. I lifted the sheets, but nothing was underneath. I glanced into the bathroom, but apart from a bottle left next to the sink and a strange smell, there were no signs that anyone had been there.

When I checked under the bed, I found a strange, battered suitcase. I opened it to find that it was empty. It did, however, have a beautiful cloth lining that was patterned with stars. There was either a number or a strange letter inside each star. It was a little odd that an otherwise shabby suitcase would have such an intricate, expensive-looking lining, but it didn't provide me with any answers, so I slipped it back under the bed.

I headed to the door more than a little disappointed. As soon as I stepped into the hallway, I could hear that Mr. McStay was still telling his story. "And this very shotgun was the one that took down the legendary Golden Hind at Weasley Point!"

I was just about to leave the room and shut the door behind me when I realized something: I'd seen the bottle next to the sink before.

I tiptoed back to the bathroom and picked up the bottle. I turned it around in my hands and then tipped it upside down. There was an engraving on the bottom that read, "Murano Brothers – Sea Couriers – Always on the crest of a wave."

That's weird, I thought. *I have a Murano Brothers bottle back home in my collection of treasures.* I sighed. *So what? There are probably hundreds of them.*

I decided that it was time to leave. I crept downstairs to where Aiby was still listening patiently to Mr. McStay. I managed to drag her out of the inn by promising the innkeeper we would return to hear his story about the Great Salmon of '92 later in the week.

We proceeded toward the parsonage in the hopes that Reverend Prospero might know where Mr. Everett was. Everything was so quiet that I could hear the choir practicing in the church. As we drew closer to the church, I told Aiby about the bottle I'd found in the bathroom, and that it was similar to the one I'd found on the beach. But before I got a chance to tell her about the riddle, Aiby fainted right into my arms.

Chapter SIXTEEN

A FAINTING SPELL, MEB THE DRESSMAKER, & THE BEACH

"Aiby! Aiby!" I cried. I held her in my arms, trying to wake her up. Just then, Meb the dressmaker saw us and hurried over to help.

"I'll go get the doctor," I said to her.

"No, Finley," Meb said. "Let's bring her inside so she can lie down for a few minutes. She probably just has sunstroke or something."

Carefully, we laid her on Meb's couch. As we sat over her, Meb fanned her with a piece of cloth.

A minute or two later, Aiby opened her eyes. She looked at me and then at Meb, who was still waving the makeshift fan over Aiby's face.

"What happened?" Aiby asked. "Where am I?"

"You passed out," I told her.

Aiby blinked hard. "I fainted?"

I nodded.

Meb handed Aiby a glass of orange juice. "Has it happened to you before?" she asked.

Aiby slowly sipped the juice. "No," she said groggily. "How did it happen?"

"Do you remember anything?" I asked.

"No," she said. "All I remember is hearing the choir sing — then everything went black."

She slowly stood up from the sofa. She wavered slightly on her long legs, but she managed to stay upright.

I told Meb who Aiby was and where she lived. "How are you two intending to get home?" Meb asked.

"My bike," I said.

Meb frowned. "That doesn't sound very safe," she said. "Would you like a ride in my car, instead?"

It wasn't a bad idea considering that Aiby had just passed out, but I couldn't just leave my bicycle behind. Bike theft wasn't common in Applecross, but I didn't want to risk losing my only means of transportation.

"Just take Aiby home," I said.

Aiby kept looking at me as though she wanted me to understand what she was thinking.

"Finley," Aiby whispered. "The bottle."

"The bottle?" I said. "What about it?"

"We need to go where you found it," Aiby said.

"Do you mean the beach where Baelanch Ba Road curves around?" I asked. She nodded. "Why?"

"Because I think we should," she said through clenched teeth.

Obviously I was missing something. I looked at Meb, who simply shrugged her shoulders. "Baelanch Ba curves on the way to Burnt Beach, right?" Meb said. "I can take you both there, if you like."

Aiby nodded. I nodded as well, not wanting to get glared at again. I'd have to risk leaving my bike behind for a little while.

* * *

Aiby and I were walking across the beach about fifty feet apart in search of clues. Patches trotted back and forth between us, occasionally veering off to chase a seagull.

"Where exactly did you find the bottle?" Aiby shouted over to me.

I snorted. "I have no idea!" I said. "How could I remember the exact spot?"

"Jeez, Finley!" she said. "What do you mean you can't remember?"

"The tide changes the beach every day," I explained.

"And it's not like there are fixed landmarks or anything to give me a point of reference."

Meb waited for us back by the road. She seemed amused by our strange request to be brought to the beach, so she gave us half an hour to patrol the beach. She insisted that she take Aiby home afterward, and then drop me off back at my bike.

I was starting to suspect that Aiby wasn't telling me the whole truth. I felt persuaded by her story about the shop, the keys, the seven families, and all that stuff, but she'd barely said a word about the Askells. In fact, when I had mentioned the name, she'd insisted on leaving the river and returning to the village to speak to Mr. Everett right away. And now that I'd told her about the bottle in the Dutchman's room and the one I'd found on the beach, here we were combing the beach entirely on her whim.

I kind of felt like I was a puppet in Aiby's hands. Even though I knew I was being played, I still enjoyed my time with her. I only believed half of what she had told me so far, but I had no choice but to accept things as they were. I mean, I couldn't just walk away — my curiosity would never have allowed me to leave with so many unanswered questions.

I stared out at the sun. It was starting to sink below the horizon. My shadow had lengthened, and it looked like it was trying to detach from my feet.

"Finley, look!" Aiby called out. She was holding up a third bottle that looked identical to the other two.

I ran over to Aiby, mirroring her look of amazement. Together, we uncorked the bottle and tipped it over. A piece of rolled-up paper fell into her hand.

She held the note open and read it out loud. "An old king held a contest between his two sons to decide who would inherit his kingdom. He told them that the son whose horse arrived at the church last would be his heir. The youngest son mounted a horse and galloped at great speed toward the church. Now I ask you, giant: why did the youngest son become king?"

"Another mysterious riddle in a bottle," I said, shaking my head.

"What does it mean?" Aiby asked.

"No idea," I said.

As I struggled to figure out the riddle, I heard Meb yelling for help.

Chapter
SEVENTEEN

A MADMAN,
HIS MASTER,
& THE AWAKENING

Aiby and I sprinted toward Meb. As we got closer, I saw a man standing next to her. He was stocky and had a big, bushy beard. Then I saw that he was also holding a strange knife to Meb's neck. It looked incredibly sharp and had small gems set into its hilt. I immediately knew it had to be a magical item.

Meb was clearly terrified. The man had one of her arms twisted behind her back and he was speaking angrily in a strange language. The more he yelled, the angrier he seemed to get.

"Who is that man?" I said. "Do you recognize him, Aiby?"

When I got no response, I turned to see that Aiby

had vanished. "Great," I muttered to myself. "What do I do now?"

I felt completely overwhelmed by the situation, but Patches didn't hesitate. He launched himself full speed at the stranger, barking wildly. He jumped with enough enthusiasm to rip the world in two — only to receive a sharp kick to his side. Patches rolled to the ground with a whimper, and then picked himself up. He began to growl again, but this time he kept his distance from the man.

I felt my blood boil at seeing the man kick my dog. The man waved his knife at us and said something I didn't understand. Meb let out another scream. I knew I had to act quickly. So I swallowed my anger and did the only thing I could think of doing: I put my hands up in the air in surrender.

"Calm down!" I said, moving toward him with my hands up.

He must be the notorious Dutchman from the McStay Inn, I realized.

"My name is Finley McPhee," I said. "What can I do to resolve this situation?"

I couldn't believe how calm I was acting. Perhaps I thought that Aiby was somewhere nearby just waiting for an opportunity to help us. Or maybe I was just worn

out from the last few days. Either way, at that moment, I realized one thing: once I graduated from school, I would move far, far away from the supposedly sleepy village of Applecross.

When I was about five steps from the Dutchman, he shoved Meb out of the way and pointed his knife at the bottle in my hand.

"This?" I asked him. "You want this? Then please take it!"

I threw it to the ground so that it would roll away from Meb. The Dutchman hopped over and stopped it with his boot. He picked it up, raised the bottle to the fading light, and realized it was empty.

The Dutchman started to scream at me again in his strange language. I held out the note that we found inside the bottle, hoping it would calm him down. The Dutchman tore it out of my hand, read it quickly, and then began to growl a series of horrible, guttural noises. *That's not Dutch*, I realized. *This man is a raving lunatic.*

The man motioned for both of us to walk toward Meb's car. I could hear the blade of the knife slice through the air as he jerked it toward the vehicle.

"Finley," Meb whispered from behind me. "Do you know this psycho?"

"Not really," I said. "But he seems pretty feral."

"Maybe your friend knows him," she whispered. "Where did she go, by the way?"

"Who knows," I said sourly.

The man growled and gestured for us to get in the car.

"Where are we going?" Meb asked. He stared at her blankly. Slowly, Meb said, "Where. We. Go?"

The Dutchman pointed to the hills. I immediately knew that he intended to take us to the Lily castle. I got this strange feeling that the disjointed language he spoke was the same language that was painted on the walls of the house. Don't ask me why, but at the time it all made sense.

Getting into the car turned out to be a difficult process. The car was small and only had two doors. He gestured for Meb to sit in the driver's seat. Then he made me climb into the back while he held the knife to my neck. Then he climbed in, too.

Before closing the door I yelled, "Patches, go home!" My dog tilted his head in a doubtful expression.

"Patches, get out of here!" I yelled at the top of my lungs. "Go. Home. Now!"

Patches took off running down the path.

Good dog, I thought. I hoped he would go back to the farm and get help, but judging by the way he was

running with his tail between his legs, he was probably just scared.

Meb started the engine. A strange beeping sound filled the car. The Dutchman's knife tightened against my neck. I calmly used my hands to explain that he needed to put on his seat belt, but he refused to buckle.

The beeping continued all the way to Lily castle. When we arrived, the lunatic finally gave us permission to get out the car.

With the crimson red of the setting sun washing over the castle, the ruins appeared even more intimidating than they had the day before. The elongated shadows from the skeletal tree branches traced strange symbols on the crumbling walls. The woods seemed even more oppressive in the darkness. Our captor's constant, violent yelling didn't help improve the mood, either.

The Dutchman forced us inside the castle. Once we were in the living room, he forced us to sit down on the floor. As I sat there, I considered the possibility that the Dutchman had been the one who'd recently used the fireplace. But if he were hiding out in the castle, then why had he rented a room at the McStay Inn?

"What do we do now?" Meb asked as soon as the man had moved away from us.

Before I could answer, the Dutchman yelled some

words in a commanding tone. He moved the knife slowly through the air as if he were tracing a symbol. My legs started to feel heavier.

"We just wait," I whispered, sounding much calmer than I felt. I tried to lift one leg, but it took all my strength to move it. It was the same with my arms. It felt like the pull of gravity had gotten stronger.

"Finley!" Meb cried. "Why can't I move?!"

"He's imprisoned us somehow," I said. "Don't fight it — the more I struggle, the harder it gets to move."

I peered around the room for something that might help, but it was too dark to see much. Above the chimney, where I'd seen the blazing pyramid the day before, there was a different drawing now — a much bigger one. A skull. Below the skull were four letters that wiggled like worms.

"Can you see those letters moving?" I whispered to Meb.

She looked at them. "Oh, dear," she muttered.

At least I'm not going crazy, I thought.

Suddenly, the four letters shifted their order into a recognizable word: LILY.

That can't be good, I thought.

"I think your friend is the one he's looking for," Meb murmured.

I nodded slowly. I glanced at our kidnapper. He was standing in a corner and seemed to be waiting for something to happen. He watched us with his wild eyes, and his face had an expression on it that was every bit as terrifying as the knife he held in his hand.

If we had any hope, it all depended on Aiby — I knew she was somewhere nearby. When we had first climbed into the car with the Dutchman, I was sure I saw my bicycle lift itself off the ground through the rear-view mirror.

At first, I was angry that Aiby had lied to me again. She obviously had more than the Cloak of Invisibility's label after all! But I couldn't help but smile as I watched her follow us on my bike.

I just hoped that Aiby knew what she was doing. I had to trust her — and her magical objects. I hoped her father would arrive at any moment armed with a whole arsenal of magical marvels and overwhelm this madman.

But neither Aiby nor her father arrived. Instead, someone far more terrifying appeared. I first felt his presence in the sudden drop in temperature. I began to shiver uncontrollably as the room was consumed with a profound silence.

Meb noticed it, too, as did the Dutchman. I'm certain

I saw a glimmer of fear glowing in his crazed eyes. It made me wonder what a nutcase like him could possibly be afraid of.

The letters on the chimney started to sparkle. Then I heard a furious flapping of wings. Then the sound of footsteps on the floor above us. Finally, the wood steps of the staircase in the room next to us creaked under the weight of someone descending.

The Dutchman hurried to take out the bottle and the message from his pockets. He scurried to the bottom of the staircase in the next room, and then stopped. From where I was sitting, I could only see his back. The footsteps coming down the stairs halted.

"Have you found the third riddle?" the stranger asked in sharp, formal English.

The Dutchman uttered a few unintelligible words. Then I heard the bottle smash against the floor

"And do you know the answer?" the stranger asked.

In a tone of voice that brought shivers to my spine, the Dutchman spoke in short bursts. Then he let out one long, furious rant. Despite stretching my neck out as much as I could, I could only make out the broken glass and the Dutchman's back.

"Did you go to the farm?" the stranger asked.

The farm? I thought. *Which farm does he mean?*

"You have all three bottles now?" the stranger said. Then, after a long pause, "Good. You don't need to kill anyone else, then."

All three bottles? I could barely think. If each bottle contained a riddle, then we had just picked up one on the beach, one was inside the bottle in room nineteen at the McStay Inn, and the other one had to be the first bottle I'd found.

"The bottle I took home," I murmured. "To the farm. *My* farm."

Cold anxiety gripped me. I desperately tried to stand, but I couldn't even shift my weight to one side.

"Now that you have all three riddles," the stranger said, "it's time for the awakening."

"Who do they want to wake up?" Meb asked, startling me. In my adrenaline-soaked haze, I'd completely forgotten that she was next to me.

"I don't know," I said in a small voice.

The mysterious visitor began to ascend the stairs. I heard his footsteps pass along the ceiling. Then there was silence. Then more silence. Suddenly, the Dutchman made a guttural noise that was beyond terrifying. I heard him moving something. Then we saw him light up some flares. Once again there was silence.

A few moments later I heard a crack, then a rustling

sound. It sounded like a tape recorder was playing. "Finley," Meb whispered, "we have to get out of here."

I'd never agreed more with anyone in my entire life. But I couldn't escape — my legs still felt as heavy as rocks. I wondered why Aiby hadn't come to help us.

The rustling sound in the other room was getting louder. Then I heard a recording of a church choir singing. My eyes nearly burst out of my head. I'd heard that song earlier that afternoon when it was being sung by the choir of Applecross!

What is the name of that song, I thought. *Come on, Finley — think!*

I thought back to what the reverend had said several days before. I was asking him about the Lily family while he was busy preparing the score for afternoon choir practice. He had been angry at the choirmaster's song choice because it was about Oberon and Puck and other so-called pagan creatures . . .

That's it! I remembered.

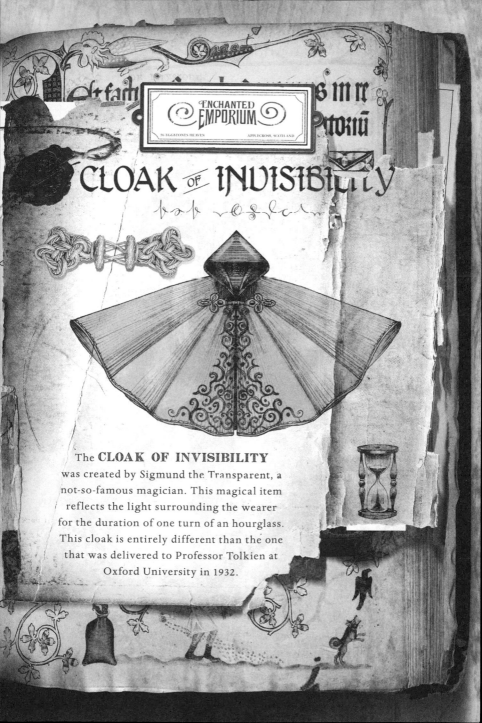

CLOAK OF INVISIBILITY

The **CLOAK OF INVISIBILITY**
was created by Sigmund the Transparent, a
not-so-famous magician. This magical item
reflects the light surrounding the wearer
for the duration of one turn of an hourglass.
This cloak is entirely different than the one
that was delivered to Professor Tolkien at
Oxford University in 1932.

Chapter
EIGHTEEN

AIBY,
THE GIANT,
& AN OLD SONG

*T*he song is called *"The Giants of the Sea!"* I remembered. *That's what Reverend Prospero called it, anyway.* It was a languid tune, but its heavy bass tones seemed to come from the depths of the earth itself. The longer it was being played, the more it freaked me out.

"Finley?" Meb whimpered. "What is happening?"

I shook my head. "I don't know," I said. "The only thing I know for sure is that they're crazy."

As if on cue, the Dutchman walked back into the living room and then disappeared into the kitchen. He returned a moment later only to disappear back into the other room again.

The song stopped playing. The end of the tape made

a slapping noise. Then, shortly afterward, it started up again. It was the same song.

I heard the Dutchman speak a series of strange words in a solemn tone of voice. The ground beneath us began to shake. The walls and ceiling began to warp, causing flakes of plaster to peel away and drop to the ground. I felt myself being shifted by an invisible force.

The castle was growing.

Cracks appeared all over the floor. The chimney snapped in two, sending down a shower of plaster and brick. The recorded choir of Applecross continued to sing their dirge while the Dutchman chanted his dismal words.

A sudden tremor knocked me over and left me groping among the flakes of plaster. When I realized that my legs and arms were no longer heavy, I jumped to my feet and shook off the debris. I glanced around, desperately searching for a way to escape.

"Meb!" I called, trying to locate her through the falling dust.

"Finley! Help!"

I heard her, but I couldn't see her. I ran toward her voice. We found each other and then ran away as fast as we could. We burst through the brambles outside. The thorns ripped our clothing and scratched us, but we

didn't slow down. Cold air filled my throat as I took in gasping breaths.

"What's happening in there?!" Meb cried as I pulled her along with me.

"It's waking up!" I cried.

Meb's eyes went wide. "What is waking up?" she asked.

"Something big!" I said.

I saw the castle walls start to split. Then the wooden roof snapped open like a rib cage. I could still hear the choir of Applecross and the Dutchman's raving voice through all the chaos and noise.

Meb and I plunged into the woods. Once we were safely inside, we stopped to catch our breath. I wanted to keep running, but it felt like there was some magnetic force keeping me close to that castle.

I'd once heard that fear can be more addictive than happiness — that horror stimulates the mind in a way that makes it impossible to look away. Well, it's true. A part of me kept wanting to run away as fast as I could, but the bigger part insisted that I stay and watch what was about to happen. It seemed to be the case for Meb, as well.

"Are you seeing this?" Meb whispered.

From the ruins of the Lily castle, a figure began to

appear. When it emerged, it looked to be ten times the size of a normal man. It was hunched over and jagged on the sides. It looked like a giant made of brick, earth, roots, and metal. Fragments of wallpaper dotted its huge shoulders. It had a tiny head, but its enormous arms and legs were still half-trapped underground.

"What is that?!" Meb cried.

Something that should have stayed asleep, I thought. *A giant made of castle and earth.*

The giant was shaking bricks off its body like Patches shaking water off after a swim. Then the choir music stopped. However, the terrifying voice of the Dutchman continued to chant. At that moment, I wanted to be somewhere else. Tucked in bed, fast asleep, at the stream, or even at school. *Anywhere but here,* I thought.

I heard a rustle of leaves nearby. "Aiby!" I shouted as she emerged from the woods. I scowled at her. "Where the heck have you been?!"

"I've been nearby," she said nervously.

"Why didn't you try to help us?!" I shouted.

"I couldn't come too close," she said. She pointed to what remained of the castle. "The choir music kept me away. The music is what made me faint earlier today in the village."

Aiby crouched down between me and Meb. She

smiled, as though everything was fine now that she had explained her absence. She glanced at the giant. It was ripping apart the web of creeping ivy that still held it down.

"Why does music make you faint?" I asked.

"Not just any music," Aiby said. "It's only that particular song. I didn't recognize it earlier today in the village. I just didn't imagine . . ."

"Imagine what?" I asked.

Aiby looked like she was in a trance. "That someone would have actually found the giant," she said.

The giant howled, shaking the ground beneath us.

I grabbed Aiby by her shoulders. "Aiby, what are you talking about?!" I cried.

Aiby sighed. "That song is our cursed family anthem," she said. "It's the same song that caused my ancestor, Reginald, to become shipwrecked here in Applecross. It's also the reason why I didn't come to help you and Meb earlier. They know what they're doing. If anyone from the Lily family hears that song — even just a few notes of it — they immediately fall into a deep sleep."

I looked at Aiby with a crooked smile. "Oh, right, of course," I said sarcastically. "Don't worry, it happens to the best of us."

"The song is linked to that thing, too!" Aiby insisted,

pointing to the struggling creature. "In the past, the Lily family had some . . . disagreements with giants. And now it seems they've found out about it."

"They?" I asked.

"Someone who wishes to do us harm," Aiby said.

"The famous Askells?" I asked.

Aiby shook her head. She pointed to the Dutchman. He was standing atop a mound of debris with his arms outstretched toward the giant. "He isn't an Askell," she said. "The Askells are tall and blond. Every single one of them."

"Then who is he?" I asked.

"His real name is Unther Farla," Aiby said. "Before he went insane, he was a carpenter in Rotterdam. Something must have happened to him. No sane person would ever enter into a contract with the Spirits of Rancour. I mean, just look at him. He's obviously lost his mind — the language he's speaking is a dead one."

The giant lifted its head toward the sky. It gave out another terrifying roar.

"What will happen now?" asked Meb.

"Farla's trying to gain control over him," Aiby said.

"Control?" I repeated.

"If you pose three riddles to a giant and it cannot answer correctly, then it will become your slave," Aiby

said. "At least until someone else stumps it with another set of three riddles. Or you die."

We could hear the Dutchman reading out the first of the three riddles.

"What's he saying now?" Meb asked.

We huddled close together. "It's a riddle about two children who are born on the same day from the same mother," Aiby translated.

"You can understand the language?" I asked.

"Of course," Aiby said. "Anyone who sells magical objects has to be fluent in all of the Spirit languages."

I thought about making a sarcastic comment, but decided I'd rather know what the Dutchman was saying.

As the Dutchman raised his voice, Aiby translated the final part of the riddle. "Now I ask you: how many children are there?"

"And the giant has to give its answer now?" Meb asked.

"If it knows the answer to the riddle, then Farla will die," Aiby whispered.

"Then what would happen?" I asked.

"The giant will be free," Aiby said.

The giant bellowed and struck its chest with its rocky arms. "It doesn't know the answer," Aiby explained.

"So now what?" I asked.

"Farla has to tell the giant the answer," Aiby said. "Then he has to give the second riddle to the giant."

The Dutchman began speaking again. He gave the solution to the first riddle, and then read out the second. Aiby translated the story of the four men and the woman, which I already knew.

"Now I ask you this," Aiby translated, "why did the woman stay dry?"

"She's in a casket," I said. Aiby nodded.

Once again, the giant battered its chest with its fists and bellowed, unable to determine the answer. The Dutchman began to read out the riddle about the king and the two sons.

"If the giant doesn't know the answer to this riddle either, then what kind of orders could this Farla guy give it?" I asked.

"Anything at all," Aiby said. "The command will last as long as Farla lives."

I didn't know which outcome was better. On the one hand, a freed giant was pretty terrifying, but Unther Farla controlling a giant seemed even worse.

We remained rooted to the spot, listening to the third riddle being read. "Now I ask you," Aiby translated, "why did the youngest son become king?"

The giant hesitated. It arched its back to stand taller.

"It knows the answer!" I said excitedly.

The giant released a low howl. It shook off a couple of rocks that were still clinging to its shoulders. Then it bent down toward the ground and propped itself up on its elbows a few feet away from the Dutchman.

"No, it doesn't know the answer," Aiby said. "Now it's in Unther Farla's power."

I frowned. "That's pretty unlucky for the giant. It's been locked underground for two centuries and now that it's finally free, it has to take orders from a complete lunatic."

"Shh!" Aiby hissed. "Let me hear what Unther is ordering it to do!"

We listened. Aiby suddenly sprang to her feet.

"What's wrong?" I asked.

"Unther ordered the giant to destroy the Enchanted Emporium!" she cried.

The giant bellowed and the ground trembled beneath us as the giant's fist smashed into the ground. The Dutchman yelled back.

"Look!" I shouted. "Something's happening!"

The giant grabbed the Dutchman and lifted him off the ground. We could see him kicking wildly as he tried to escape the giant's grip.

"I don't believe it!" Aiby whispered.

"What?" I asked.

"Unther Farla doesn't know the answer to the last riddle, either," she said. "So the command isn't valid!"

The giant opened its enormous mouth. It was crammed full of razor-sharp teeth. The giant lifted the Dutchman over its head and released its grip.

And just like that, Unther Farla was gone forever.

Now the giant was free to leave its underground prison. It jumped over what was left of the ruined castle and plunged into the woods with alarming agility. It ran right past us, missing us by just a few yards. It brushed the trees aside like they were twigs, leaving a path of broken trunks behind it.

The ground rumbled and shuddered with each step it took, making it nearly impossible to keep my balance. We headed away from the giant and finally emerged in the fields belonging to the Dogberry farm. From there, with the meadows and fields below us, we could see the giant's outline silhouetted against the starlit sky.

"It looks like it's heading toward the sea," I said.

"Go, gentle giant. Go!" Aiby said, watching the giant slowly make its way toward the sea. "You're free now. Return to your home beneath the waves!"

The giant came to a sudden stop near the coastal road. Aiby fell silent and her shoulders sagged. I can't say how long the giant stayed there staring out at sea, but the entire time I could hear Aiby muttering under her breath. "Please return home. I beg of you. Please return home."

Then the giant began to turn around. I could see tears running down Aiby's face as she watched the giant head north toward the Enchanted Emporium.

Chapter
NINETEEN

GAE BULG,
CUCHALAINN,
& ME

Meb's fingers gripped the steering wheel as she slammed her foot down hard on the accelerator. The car bumped and rattled over the field, shaking violently every time the giant took another step.

"Faster, faster!" Aiby said.

"Hold on tight!" Meb cried. She cranked the wheel to the right and rode over the lip of a ditch. The car soared through the air and landed on the coastal road. Once we were running along its smooth surface, it felt like driving on clouds compared to the field.

Aiby poked her head out the window. Her eyes followed the giant's outline as it headed toward the promontory of Burnt Beach. It looked like a walking black mountain.

"Are you sure it's heading toward the Emporium?" I asked, clinging to my seat.

Meb turned the car around a bend so sharply that the tires squealed. It was a miracle that Aiby didn't fly out of the window. I grabbed her arm to hold her inside the car.

Aiby held her hands to the sides of her head. "I told you!" she said. "We've had some disagreements with the giants in the past!"

"Like what?" I asked.

Aiby sighed. Judging by the expression on her face, this was her most difficult confession yet. "Long ago, a family of Wandering Giants neglected to —"

"Hold on!" Meb cried.

We were tossed against one side of the car and then the other. Aiby continued. "The giants refused to pay their bill, so one member of the Lily family challenged them to a riddle competition. My ancestor won, so he got to take control of one of the giants. He said he would keep the giant hidden away until the rest of the giants finally paid their bill."

"I'm guessing the others didn't pay the debt," I said.

"No," Aiby said. "Even worse, they were so angry that they cast a curse on the Lily family: we only have to hear a few notes of their anthem, "The Giants of the Sea," and we immediately fall into a deep sleep."

I guess that's what happens when you take a giant hostage, I thought.

I glanced out the window. It was thrilling to be driving at top speed with the black sheen of the sea to our left and the rolling green hills to our right. I gazed out over Applecross as it stretched out behind us.

"But how does the giant know that the Enchanted Emporium is on the promontory?" I asked.

"Giants are magical creatures," Aiby said. "They can sense and track magic like a bloodhound sniffs out a fox."

"What is it going to do when it gets there?" I asked. "I mean, it doesn't have to carry out the Dutchman's instructions anymore, right?"

Aiby nodded. "Right," she said. "But if it really is the giant that was imprisoned by my ancestor, then it's probably pretty angry with the Lily family right now."

"I can imagine," I said. "What about the writing that moved on the walls?"

"What?" Aiby asked. "What writing?"

"At the castle," I said. "There were strange symbols on the walls that moved when you looked at them."

Aiby narrowed her eyes. "You saw the words move?" she asked.

"Well, yeah," I said.

"I saw it, too," Meb said from the driver's seat. She

191

slowed down to turn a corner, then revved the engine and accelerated down the road.

Something passed overhead. I poked my head out the window to look. A strange flock of birds were flying in formation toward Applecross.

"Yes!" Aiby cried when she saw them. "Dad must have heard about what's going on."

"So?" I asked, watching the birds make their way toward the village.

"Dad sent the Dream Weavers to Applecross," Aiby explained. "Each one of them carries a golden thread in its beak. Together, the strands form a Web of Dreams. Once it's placed over the village, everyone beneath it will fall into a deep sleep." She turned to look at me. "But don't worry, it's only to keep the villagers from panicking about what they might see tonight."

"You put them to sleep," I said.

Aiby nodded and smiled. "And make them dream that everything is fine," she said.

We went past the last bend in the road before the promontory. Meb's speedy driving had allowed us to gain some ground on the giant. It had just reached the road sign that marked the start of Burnt Beach.

A bunch of startled seagulls flap into the air and fly away from the giant as it walked down Reginald Bay.

192

Meb parked the car at the beginning of the promontory. We all jumped out and began running after that monstrous creature.

I soon saw Mr. Lily. He was standing halfway between the forest and the rocks with his legs planted wide apart. He was dressed in a comical outfit of jeans, running shoes, and a medieval knight's breastplate. His long blond hair poked out of an ancient helmet, and he held a round shield in one hand and a spear with a jagged tip in the other. Immediately I realized that Mr. Lily was planning to face the giant before it reached the Enchanted Emporium.

As soon as Mr. Lily saw the giant up close, he wavered indecisively between the rocks and the forest. The expression on his face reminded me of a child seeing an unusual-looking insect for the first time.

Mr. Lily was no taller than the giant's knee, but he still stood his ground. He raised his spear at the giant, and his voice boomed out like a Homeric hero: "Go back where you came from, foul creature!"

Aiby and I stopped running. "Dad, don't do it!" she cried. "You can't defend the Emporium from that thing!"

The giant picked up a nearby boulder like a basketball and hurled it into the sea with all its might. The rock sank into the black water with a deafening splash. Then

the giant turned to face Mr. Lily and let out a gravelly roar.

"That looked like a warning shot," I said grimly.

But Mr. Lily seemed unperturbed. He raised his spear again and bellowed, "In the name of Gae Bulg, the Spear of Mortal Pain, forged out of the bones of the Coinchenn, the Terror of the Abyss, I, Locan Lily, command you to return from where you came and to do it now!"

The air was saturated with the stench of rotten organic matter. I realized the putrid smell was coming from the giant, which only made it seem more terrifying. Next to the giant, Aiby's father looked about as big as an ear of corn.

The giant took a step closer to Mr. Lily. Aiby turned as pale as the moon. I had to grab her by the arm and hold her back so she didn't throw herself between the two of them.

"You shall not pass!" Locan Lily yelled.

The giant roared and took another step. It bent at the waist and reached for another boulder.

"Dad!" Aiby screamed.

"Get down!" I shouted.

I lunged at Aiby and pushed her out of the way just in time. A huge rock hurled by the giant landed right where

Aiby had been a moment earlier. I felt the impact before I heard it. The rush of air alone nearly knocked the breath out of me.

I rolled onto my side, gasping. When I got to my feet again, I saw that the situation had gotten even worse. Locan Lily was lying in a pile of rocks like a broken doll. His helmet had fallen and rolled away, and his spear had become wedged into the ground.

"Dad!" Aiby screamed, leaping to her feet.

I felt a second powerful whoosh of air above my head. When I looked up, I saw the giant moving over us and continuing on its way toward the Enchanted Emporium. A swarm of seagulls were circling around the giant's head, continually trying to peck at it. The giant swatted at them like they were flies and kept moving down the bay.

Meb had run to help Locan Lily. Aiby was already lifting his head up. He opened his eyes. A stream of blood dripped from his lips.

"Oh, Dad," Lily said, tears streaming down her face.

"I'm fine," Mr. Lily moaned. "That thing sure was . . . big, huh?"

"You shouldn't have tried to stop him!" Aiby wailed. "What were you thinking?"

Meb pulled out a small bottle of water from her

purse and gave Mr. Lily a drink. She gently ran her hand over his body to see whether he had broken anything.

"Someone — ouch!" Mr. Lily cried. "Someone had to try to stop him."

"Not you, Dad!" Aiby said. "It's not your job! You're just a researcher — not the protector of Enchanted Emporium."

I gazed out at the bay, and it started to feel like I was on an alien planet. I could see the back of the giant set against the shivering black sea, a crown of whirling seagulls over its head, and its terrible stench still permeated the area.

I glanced at the spear that was wedged into the ground between two petrified trunks of wood. My heart started to beat in my chest like a drum, and I'm not exaggerating — it really did sound like a drum. It had a slow, thudding rhythm to it. A marching rhythm, like the sound of an advancing army.

I walked toward the spear without even realizing what I was doing and yanked it out of the ground. It felt light and balanced in my hands. I could see that it had been cut from a single bone and then coated with ornate metalwork. The bladed tip had jagged teeth that sparkled menacingly in the moonlight.

I found myself studying each tooth, one by one. In

that moment, the spear seemed like the most fascinating thing I'd ever laid eyes on. I tilted it back and forth in my hands. I could feel my heart beat in time with the subtle shimmering of the bladed edge.

"Gae Bulg," I whispered. Upon speaking the spear's real name, it sent a burst of energy into my body. My spine straightened and I squeezed my fingers around the spear. I closed my eyes and saw one of the monsters of the abyss before me, the Coinchenn of Irish mythology. Then the hero, Cuchalainn, appeared to me in the eye of a storm. Then I saw a flash of an immense battlefield where the dead warriors sang a gloomy song.

"Finley?" Aiby called, pulling me back to reality. "What are you doing?"

Slowly, Aiby's face came into focus. Then I looked at Meb, who was kneeling next to Mr. Lily. In that moment, Locan looked pathetic in my eyes.

"This is mine," I said, lifting the spear and holding it out in front of me.

"Finley, what is going on with you?" Aiby asked.

"Pass me the shield," I said.

Propelled by an unseen force, the wooden shield rolled to my feet. I bent down, picked it up, and attached it to my forearm in one deft movement.

I turned toward the giant. It had reached the end

of the path at the point where it curved toward the red house.

In a voice that was not my own, but belonging to the heroes who had handled the weapon and shield long before me, I said: "It's time for all of you to witness how a real warrior does battle!"

THE WEB of DREAMS

The Web of Dreams is formed by a tangle of golden threads
that can be lifted and transported only by Dream Weavers, or
specially trained birds. When carefully positioned over a house,
the Web of Dreams will protect the inhabitants from unpleasant
noises and harmful influences while they dream peacefully.

Chapter
TWENTY

ANCIENT HEROES,
FOUL-MOUTHED GIANTS,
& DOUG

I ran through the woods, jumping from rock to rock like a jackrabbit. When I reached the edge, I slid on my back down the smooth stones in an attempt to catch up to the giant. I kept close to the north side of the cove that was closest to the Enchanted Emporium. The giant was approaching from the spot where I had first parked Jules's bicycle nearly a week ago.

The giant was only about ten steps away from the Enchanted Emporium. It wouldn't take it long to get there, even with the crown of seagulls that continued to peck at its head.

But I wasn't worried.

I saw the huge form of the giant approaching on my left side. I wanted to get between it and the Enchanted Emporium in time to launch my attack. I ignored the scratches I was getting from slipping down the stones and used my spear to propel me even faster.

The giant's thumping footsteps echoed around the entire bay. Each time it placed a foot on the ground, all of the oval-shaped rocks rattled and shook like decorations on a Christmas tree.

But I wasn't afraid. After all, I was Cuchalainn, the hero of Gae Bulg. I was a legend. I was invincible.

I steadied myself, picked a spot to land, and then jumped. I landed on the roof of the red house, rolled, and landed on my feet right in front of the giant.

"Hey, you big ape!" I yelled, lifting the spear toward him.

The giant stopped. The gulls were still circling its head. I was completely engulfed by the giant's shadow. I swung the spear in one direction and then another. I twirled it in one hand, then tossed it into the air like a baton. I caught it behind my back, spun it forward, and then I pointed its tip at the giant's skull.

I squeezed the shield against me. With it held tight

to my body, I felt it begin to influence me just like the spear had.

"Scram!" the shield made me shout. "Get out of here, you bully. That's all you are — a big, lumbering, smelly, stupid bully!"

I couldn't believe what I was saying! I had a brand new vocabulary in my head of offensive words and insults — along with an undeniable desire to use them against the giant.

I let the insults flow in one long stream: "Go back where you came from and gorge on mud with the rest of your mud-loving family! Well, what are you waiting for, turnip head? I'm going to singe your backside with the righteous flames of justice! I'm ready to call on Atlas, Goliath, Etion, Enceladus, Adamastor, Aegeon, Gabbara, Artachaeus, Oromedon, Gemmagog, Fracassus, Hapmouche, Bolivorax, Gayoffo, Angoulevent, Galehaut, Mirelangaut, Roboast, Sortibrant, Mabrun, Grangousier, and Gargantua! That's right, all of them — at the same time!"

The unstoppable stream of taunting came from the shield. While the spear had belonged to an ancient Irish hero, the shield had been made as a birthday present for a jolly giant. His spirit was now fighting with the spirit of

Cuchalainn for control of my body. It felt like I was the rope in a game of tug-of-war between two gods.

The rocky giant seemed impressed by my sudden boldness — in fact, it took a step backward. "That's right, back up," I said. "And run home to your smelly mommy!"

I felt a surge of confidence and lost all my remaining restraint. "Go home! Pan licker! Welly maker! You go back to where you came from! You bean sheller, lantern maker, chicken seller — get out of here! Horse brusher, frog hunter, saucepan scrubber — get a move on it! You're nothing but a bumbling bag of brain-dead boulders! Now run away like the idiot you are!"

As it turned out, the giant had only taken a step backward so that it would be in better position for an attack. One of its fists hurtled toward the ground, but it was too slow and predictable to hit me. I easily dodged to the side and then stuck the spear into its arm. The blade tore the giant's skin open, and the jagged teeth on the tip produced a cascade of sparks.

The giant howled and jerked its arm back. Still holding the spear, I found myself flying through the air. I rotated the spear, releasing its grip on the giant's arm, and fell to the ground with a resounding thud.

Everything was blurry. I opened my eyes and found myself on the grass among some rocks. I saw movement above me and realized that the furious giant was lifting a leg, intending to stomp on me.

I didn't have time to roll out of the way. *This is it,* I thought. *This is the end. And I didn't even get to see the best moments of my life pass before my eyes.*

The giant's foot came down, blotting out all the light. For a moment, I thought I was dead. Then I felt fragments of earth falling onto my face and the pressure of the giant's foot — but I hadn't yet been crushed! I opened my eye to see that a rock had rolled next to me and wedged itself underneath the giant's foot just in time to save me.

As quick as a flash, I slid out from under the giant's sole. I'd escaped! I could see the sky above me once again. Right at that moment, I heard a bark. It was like being showered with gold.

"Patches!" I yelled. My dog was bounding courageously toward the giant. He sank his teeth into the giant's ankle like a tick attaching itself to a sheepdog. Then I saw that Patches hadn't come alone. Doug was there, too, armed with Dad's rifle.

I learned later that Doug had been the one who

rolled the stone under the giant's foot, saving my life. Pretty smart for a dumb brother.

"Doug!" I said. "My brother!"

"Leave Finley alone, you monster!" he shouted.

Then he turned toward Burnt Beach, and in a louder voice called out, "Don't worry, Wilma! Doug's here to save the day!" Doug raised the rifle. Two shots fired from its barrel.

The shots struck the giant square in the chest. Bits of rock and sparks flew in every direction. There was a long silence while the surprised giant examined its smoking chest.

At the second round of gunfire, the giant covered its ears as if the noise irritated him more than the actual bullets. All the while, Patches was nipping furiously at its ankles.

Doug reloaded and he closed the barrel with surprising ease. *Crack!* Another round shot into the air with a deafening burst. The blast hit the giant on the side of its head, tilting it. It lowered its hands from its ears and glared at Doug.

"Uh-oh," Doug said.

The giant dashed at us like a semi driving at full speed. It smashed the stones around us with its whirling

fists. Doug was tossed back against the red house, his rifle skittering away and out of his reach. Patches whimpered and cowered next to a pile of rocks and an anxious-looking seagull.

I used the distraction to crawl on my belly along the ground in search of my spear.

Where'd it go? I wondered.

Just then, I spotted the spear at the end of the path closest to the Enchanted Emporium. I made my way on my elbows along the ground as fast as I could. Just as I thought I'd reached the spear, I found myself swinging up into the air!

I saw the ground and the sky switch places like I was riding one of those nauseating circus rides. A moment later, I was staring directly into the giant's right eye. It was milky white and had no pupil.

It seemed to be examining me like a scientist studying a lab rat. Then it opened his jaws and exhaled. I was sickened by an overpoweringly foul smell.

I kicked and flailed as hard as I could in an effort to free myself. The giant threw its head back, and then held me up to take a second look, seemingly amused by my helpless writhing.

Maybe there's another way to amuse it, I thought.

"Let's make a deal!" I shouted with what little breath I had left. "I hear you giants like riddles, right?"

Its huge milky eye narrowed.

"Good! Then try this one on for size: why can't the Scotsman marry his widow's sister?"

The giant tilted its head and lifted me up in front of its eyes again.

"Well?" I said. "Do you know the answer to my riddle, or not?"

I could feel the giant's grip on me softening a little. I could actually breathe again. "I'll give you a bit more time to think about it," I shouted. "But don't you try to trick me."

"Finley, what is wrong with you?!" Doug yelled. "Get down from there, you idiot!"

I sighed. Only Doug would imagine that I was voluntarily allowing a giant to crush me to death between its hands.

"Five!" I counted. "Four!" I closed my eyes. "Three-two-one!"

The giant's fingers opened and I slipped free. I landed on the ground with my feet beneath me. I was so shocked, though, that I stumbled and fell onto my back. Doug ran over and helped me up.

"What did you do to him?" Doug asked.

I smirked. "The Scottish riddle," I said.

"Oh, right!" Doug said, pretending to understand. "Um, now what?"

I smiled at my brother. I wanted to ask him how he had known to come there to save my life. I wanted to confess that I'd lied about Aiby's name. I wanted to tell him I was impressed by his quick thinking.

But there wasn't time for any of that.

"Now I have to tell the giant the answer," I said, turning to face it.

The giant tilted its head, its milky eyes blinking at me. "The Scotsman can't marry his widow's sister because if she's a widow, then the Scotsman must already be dead!"

Silence.

Then more silence.

Did it understand my riddle? I wondered.

The giant placed a rocky palm on its forehead and let out what sounded like a sigh of disappointment. Then it shrugged its shoulders as if to say, "Oh, well" and sat noisily to the ground.

"What now," Doug asked while still scanning the horizon for his precious Wilma.

I brushed the dust off my shirt. "Don't worry, bro," I said. "I have everything under control."

I walked up to the waiting giant and stood between its legs so I could look it straight in the eyes. It gazed at me with its head tilted, waiting for the second riddle.

I gulped. *Now I have to think up another one,* I thought.

THE **SHIELD** of **AGITATION**

The Shield of Agitation was made
from the bottom half of the wooden
mug owned by Pantagruel, the infamously
foul-mouthed giant. Whoever wields this shield
inherits Pantagruel's arrogance, affinity for
insults, and all sorts of other irritating behaviors
that are sure to agitate one's enemies.

Chapter
TWENTY-ONE

A GOOD IDEA,
A BAD RIDDLE,
& AN OLD DEBT

I was terrible at thinking up riddles — even worse than I was at math or history. I'd never been able to figure one out by myself or remember any of them. It was the same way with telling jokes. I wasn't like Jackie Turbine, who could tell fifty jokes one after the other and leave you aching with laughter. For me, they just went in one ear and out the other.

So when I found myself in front of that stinking mountain of rock and earth looking at me expectantly for a second riddle, I desperately racked my brain.

But nothing came to me.

Not even one riddle.

My mind was a complete blank.

Now I could see Aiby at the top of the cove, her father's blond hair on one side and Meb's darker hair on the other. I could hear Doug a few steps behind me, too frightened to get any closer. All their eyes were on me.

I hate these tense silences, I thought. *They're only supposed to happen in films — and only then at the end.*

I heard a trickle of moving pebbles and found Patches sitting at my feet.

"Hey, buddy," I said with a smile. "You realize we're in big trouble, right?"

He returned his usual bland expression. As usual, he was fine with whatever I was talking about. I knew in that moment that there was no human in the world he would choose over me.

Or maybe it was just what I hoped was true. Maybe Patches was just hungry and wanted to go home. Thinking about this, though, bought me enough time to come up with another riddle.

"Listen, giant," I said. "What do you call . . ." I'm embarrassed to say that my voice cracked a little.

Slow down, Finley, I thought. *You still have some time left to think. You're about to tell the giant a riddle that makes absolutely no sense. It's not even a real riddle. The giant will solve it and then it'll swallow you whole, like it did with Unther Farla.*

But I didn't have another riddle to give the giant, so I gathered some courage and continued. "What do you call something that's as big as a cat, furry like a cat, has a tail like a cat, paws like a cat, whiskers like a cat, and catches mice like a cat — but isn't a cat?"

Done. I'd said it. Now it was out of my hands. All of our lives, as well as the fate of the Enchanted Emporium, now rested in the hands of the giant.

The monster tilted its head one way, and then the other. He balanced his chin on his hands. Then he gave out a long, sad sigh.

I couldn't believe it. He didn't know the answer.

Time ticked away. The silence was so profound that it seemed like the sea had frozen over and the stars had gone completely still.

"Five . . ." I said, holding out five fingers.

I waited a moment. "Four."

"Three. Two. One!"

The giant shrugged. So I gave him the answer. "A she-cat."

"Seriously?" Doug said. "A she-cat? That doesn't even make any sense! We're all dead."

I gulped.

The giant began to shake its shoulders. It opened its mouth in a strange way and let out a gravelly sound.

215

I couldn't believe it — the giant was laughing!

The monster bent over and patted me on the shoulder, which by some miracle didn't send me tumbling off the cliff. Then it motioned for me to tell the final riddle.

No matter how much I rooted through my memory, I could only recall one other riddle. It was the only riddle I could remember because I'd heard it repeated twice that day and nearly died in the process. And it was a good riddle — a really tough one to solve.

"Finley?" Doug whispered anxiously. He looked as pale as a sheet.

Even the giant was starting to fidget.

"I have a riddle, Doug," I said. "Don't worry." It was true, I had a riddle in mind. There was just one problem: I didn't know the answer to it.

I lifted my eyes to meet the giant's gaze, and retold the Dutchman's third riddle about the king and his two sons as best I could.

"An old king held a contest between his two sons to decide who would get his kingdom. He told them that, um, the son whose horse arrived at the church last would be his heir. The youngest son mounted a horse and galloped at great speed toward the church. Now I ask you, giant: why did the youngest son become king?"

The giant seemed to remember the riddle from

216

before. It rested its head on its palm, once again trying to figure out the answer.

In the meantime, I tried to do the same. *Come on, Finley,* I thought. *You can do it.*

I wondered if I should ask Doug for help. After all, he had figured out the first riddle. "Doug?" I whispered. My brother didn't answer. "Doug?"

I turned to look at him and saw that he'd passed out. "Great," I muttered. It would've been kinda funny except for that fact that, you know, we were all about to die.

A king and two sons, I thought. *The last to arrive at the church on horseback will be king. The younger son takes a horse and gallops toward the church on it. So how could he win if he arrived first?*

It seemed like an impossible scenario. That meant there had to be a twist. *But what is it?* I thought.

The giant shifted its weight. I should have already started the countdown, but what was the point if I didn't know the answer?

I closed my eyes and imagined that my dad was the king, and that Doug and I were the two brothers. Doug was the eldest — and the dumb one. I was the younger, smarter one. So why would I, the smarter son, grab my horse and gallop to the church if I knew the son whose horse arrived last would become king?

The giant grunted. I could tell it was time to begin the countdown. I started very slowly. "Five."

If my horse arrived first, I thought, then Doug would win the kingdom. There's no doubt about that.

"Four."

Maybe Doug deserves the kingdom, I thought. He isn't so bad, after all. He's strong, courageous, and he's good at rugby. And he saved my life — even if he did it mostly to impress Aiby — er, Wilma.

"Three."

But that didn't matter, because the younger brother became king in the riddle, anyway, I thought. So if he had grabbed his horse and dashed toward the church, it was because . . .

"Two."

Come on, Finley, I thought. Time's up.

"One . . ."

My eyes popped open. *That's it! I realized. It was so simple. The younger brother didn't take his horse — he took his brother's horse!*

"You see, my giant friend," I said. "The younger son inherited the kingdom because he didn't ride his own horse. Instead, he took his older brother's horse and rode it to the church. That way, he was sure his own horse would arrive last. And the kingdom would be his."

The giant let out an agitated wail. Then it clumsily

lifted itself up in an immense twisting of rocky limbs. It leaned right up into my face. It was less than a step away from me, staring at me. Waiting.

Patches barked at it.

From the path above us, I heard Aiby cry out. I turned to see her running toward me along with her father and Meb.

My brother tapped me on the shoulder. "What's with the giant?" he asked.

I chuckled. Three riddles, three answers. The pact had been made. "It's waiting for my command," I said.

"Cool!" Doug said. After a moment, he added, "What are you going to make it do?"

The giant was breathing steadily, waiting for me to speak. Thanks to the Enchanted Emporium, it had been waiting underground for hundreds of years, only to be released from its prison by a crazy man with a vendetta. All because of a debt that had nothing to do with either of us.

Aiby and her father had almost reached me, but I wanted to give my command before they arrived. I didn't want to hear what they had to say, because I was going to make the decision myself.

I rested my hands on the giant's chin. "Go home, giant," I said. My voice was soft and quiet like the rustle

of tissue paper. "I command you to be free and to return to your family. I command you to never harm the Lily family, or anyone else for that matter. You've more than paid the debt to the Enchanted Emporium. No one owes anyone anything anymore."

I lowered my hands. The giant lifted its head gently.

"You're free," I repeated.

It looked around nervously, but didn't move.

"Have courage," I said.

I saw what looked like a smile on the giant's face. It turned, looked toward the sea, and started walking.

Aiby, her father, and Meb had reached me. Doug was by my side, and Patches was at my feet. Together, in silence, we watched the giant as it slowly clambered toward the sea.

When the giant reached the edge of the water, it turned around to look back at us. It raised an arm as if to wave goodbye.

Patches let out a single bark. We all waved back, even Mr. Lily. "Please don't come back!" Mr. Lily said.

Aiby was gazing out at the sea. Her eyes were brimming with tears. When she saw me looking at her, she slipped her hand into mine.

I took it and squeezed.

Patches was the only one who noticed. He lifted his

face and rested it against my leg. I couldn't tell if he was jealous or happy.

We stayed like that for a long time until the giant disappeared into the sea. My brother elbowed Aiby gently in the side. "What a crazy day, huh, Wilma?" he whispered.

Aiby shot Doug a confused glance.

I laughed.

Chapter
TWENTY-TWO

GOOD FRIENDS,
A GRAND OPENING,
& A GREAT GIFT

Thanks to the Dream Weavers, none of the villagers had any idea what had happened that night. They'd all been sleeping and dreaming, protected by the Web of Dreams that had been draped over the village.

Aiby had wanted to use the Professional Memory Removal Dust on Doug, but I persuaded her not to. My brother had saved my life. Even if he'd been dumb enough to think that a rifle was a good weapon against a rock monster, I still thought he'd earned the honor of remembering that crazy night. Besides, I'd need some leverage to convince him not to kill me once I told him that Wilma's real name was Aiby.

The next day, I returned to my duties with Reverend Prospero and the post office. I began to study the

behavior of all the villagers who had played a part in the incident. There was the choir master who'd chosen "The Giants of the Sea" for the choir to practice. And Mr. Everett had compiled the list of names that included the Lily family. Last, there was the Widow Rozenkratz, the superintendent who had failed me. Then again, that was probably all my fault.

The Dutchman's knife was never found.

No more messages in bottles turned up.

But at least no more giants appeared.

Whenever I could, I still went fishing at my secret place, but I began to enjoy my solitude at the river less and less. In all honesty, I just couldn't stop myself from thinking about Aiby whenever we were apart.

A few days after the giant episode, everything was ready for the grand opening of the Enchanted Emporium. The first few guests started to arrive in the village. Soon, people from all over the world began to fill the streets of Applecross. They examined shop windows and gathered in small groups to chat. Some of them greeted each other warmly while others barely spoke a word to anyone. Regardless, the McStay Inn didn't have a single empty room for the entire weekend, and the kitchens were constantly ladling out cold soup and dry leg of lamb.

The Lily family had generously decided to invite the whole village to the grand opening. I delivered the invitations myself. They read:

You are cordially invited
to the grand opening of
the Enchanted Emporium.
Just bring this letter — and your curiosity!

I even persuaded my parents to attend.

Immediately, villagers and visitors alike began to gossip about what the party would be like. People whispered about a fabulous fireworks display that was sure to occur. Three submersible sailing vessels were seen floating in Reginald Bay, leading everyone to speculate that mysterious marine adventurers would be in attendance. The women of Applecross mobbed Mrs. Ivana's beauty salon, and the line of men at the village barber shop trailed out the front door and down the street.

Meb was constantly busy repairing the villagers' best clothes. The McBlacks were the only ones not to show their faces that weekend. The last time anyone had seen them was for the funeral of poor Mr. Dogberry. I noted that each of the four undertakers wore black clothing, but that was probably just a coincidence.

The grand opening was scheduled to start at 5:17 in the afternoon, but Aiby asked me to come a little earlier to give her a hand with some last minute preparations.

As I pedaled my bike, Patches followed behind me. I'd pinned up the right leg of my dress pants so they wouldn't rub against the chain and get grease on them. I held a small bunch of flowers that I had picked by the river. I tried to carry them lightly so they wouldn't get shaken up while I biked, but I ended up brandishing them like a club whenever I hit a bump in the road.

At the turn in the road, I could see that Mr. Lily had done a great job hiding all traces of the episode with the giant. All the damage had been cleverly concealed, and Burnt Beach was filled with new shrubs, oak trees, and fresh green saplings. In the distance, just beyond the Enchanted Emporium, I saw a hot air balloon anchored to the ground.

I hopped off my bike and leaned it against a rock. As soon as Aiby saw me walking toward her, she ran over and hugged me. She looked so beautiful that I could hardly breathe. There were a thousand things I wanted to tell her, but instead I held out the scrubby looking bouquet of flowers I'd picked and blurted out the first complimentary thing that came to mind: "Wow, Aiby! I almost didn't recognize you."

It was true, in a way. She wore a gray dress that was tied at the waist with a large bow. Her sparkling ballet pumps must have been magical since they were almost blindingly bright. Her hair was tied back in a long ponytail, and she wore tiny pearl earrings. She looked like a real princess come to life. But underneath it all, I knew she had the heart of a rebel.

"Flowers? For me?" she purred. "You shouldn't have, Finley!" Judging by the way she held the wilted bouquet to her nose, I knew it had been the right choice. I let her take me by the hand and lead me to the Emporium as if she were showing me the way for the first time.

Meb was near the front door. She waved and smiled. She looked elegant in a short dress patterned with blue and yellow flowers. I had to admit that she was a gifted dressmaker.

The Lily family had set up a series of tables against the cliff, and all of them were loaded with plates of food. A light sea breeze played with the ends of the checked tablecloths, making me wonder if they were actually flying carpets in disguise.

"Welcome, Finley," Aiby's father said in his strangely detached manner.

I nodded at him. "Hi, Mr. Lily," I said. "Hey, Meb."

Meb smiled and pointed out that I still had my pants

pinned up on my right leg. I blushed and bent down to remove the pins, hoping no one would see how red my face was.

"It looks like you're all here," Mr. Lily said enigmatically. "Shall we begin?"

Aiby nodded and disappeared into the shop. A moment later, she emerged holding two small but ornate wooden boxes.

"Dad and I have talked a lot over the past few days," Aiby said. She looked at her father before continuing. He returned her gaze, then glanced at me and Meb. Then he nodded.

Aiby handed one of the boxes to Meb, and then gave the other one to me. "These are gifts for saving the Enchanted Emporium and our family," she said. "We want you both to know how much we appreciate all that you've done for us."

Meb and I looked at each other uncertainly.

"Finley, my daughter said that you were able to read the incantation," Mr. Lily said.

I wasn't sure what he was referring to. "At the old castle," Aiby added. "You know, the letters that moved around on their own."

"Oh, that," I said, smiling. "We read it, yeah, but we didn't understand a single word of it."

The Lily family laughed. They seemed to be relieved. But it was a lie. I'd been able to read their family name written underneath the skull. I decided to keep that fact to myself — for now.

"It takes practice, like everything," Aiby said. She motioned for us to open the boxes.

I nodded at Meb to open hers first. The box contained a golden key with a stem that was shaped like a bee.

"We're asking you to become an associate of our Emporium, Meb," Aiby explained. "We need someone who can repair things, someone who knows how to tinker with magical objects that are broken or no longer work. We want that person to be you."

Meb didn't say anything, but she held the bee-shaped key to her chest and blushed.

I opened my box. It also contained a golden key, but this one had a stem shaped like a scorpion.

Aiby smiled warmly at me. "Finley, for the courage you showed against the giant, and the way that you wielded the spear and shield like you were a true champion . . ." Aiby trailed off, seemingly fighting back tears. In that moment, I wanted to tell her that she didn't need to explain anything. That it was fine, and of course I accepted her gift. But I didn't have the courage to say it in front of Meb and her father, so I just stared at the key

and waited for her to finish speaking. "We're giving you this key because we would all feel safer if you agreed to become the Enchanted Emporium's protector."

I couldn't believe my ears. I was overcome with emotion and couldn't speak — which is, after all, the simplest and the most complex kind of magic all at once.

Then again, what could be said? The Lilys were asking us to go into business with them. No, it was even more than that. It was a bond with their family, too.

"I don't know what to say," I said, which was truthful. I bent over and let Patches sniff the scorpion key to the Enchanted Emporium.

"What do you think, Patches?" I asked. "Should we accept?"

My best friend looked up at me and let out two satisfied barks.

"You heard him," I said. "We're in!"

"Me, too," Meb said.

Aiby and her father exchanged a relieved sigh.

"Okay, *now* we really are ready to open shop," they said.

And for the first time, the four of us stepped inside the Enchanted Emporium together.

THE CRICKET KEY

THE SCORPION KEY

These four golden keys have handles shaped like insects. When used simultaneously by four different owners, the keys open the entrance to the fabled Enchanted Emporium.

THE HONEYBEE KEY

THE SCARAB BEETLE KEY

Chapter
TWENTY-THREE

FOUR KEYS,
FOUR FRIENDS, &
THE LOVE OF MYSTERY

There would be no point describing word for word how the grand opening went. Needless to say, it lasted late into the night. The fireworks were set off over the sea, which made them doubly spectacular. There were more than a thousand guests, but the arsenal of magical pots and pans provided more than enough food for everyone. Many guests arrived by boat, several arrived by carriage, and one, as I mentioned earlier, showed up in a hot air balloon. There were many bizarre collectors of magical objects, young and old, male and female, and some whose age or gender I couldn't determine.

It was a celebration of different cultures, languages, and costumes from every corner of the world. I was fairly

certain that every country in the world was represented in some way that night.

Patches barked at everyone he could, without exception. He ran from table to table, shamelessly begging for scraps. By the end of the night, his belly was so full that he could only lie on his back and moan contentedly.

Doug was telling three pretty girls all about his exploits with the giant. I'd never seen him so proud and happy. I saw Mom and Dad chatting with Reverend Prospero close to the entrance of the red house.

The Lily family had asked everyone to bring their invitations with them because they had been scented with a magical perfume that allowed the guests to enter the Emporium and look around.

At first, I wondered if it was a good idea to let the residents of Applecross into a store filled with magical goods. As it turned out, seeing the store for themselves set their minds at ease and seemed to dismiss any worries they had about witchcraft and devilry they'd previously gossiped about. Most of them described it as a cross between an antique store and a bookstore.

Toward the end of the evening, one of the guests who had mostly kept to himself approached Aiby and whispered something in her ear. It was the man who had arrived by hot air balloon. His wispy mustache made him look like someone who had long contemplated the most profound questions of existence for many years.

He chatted with Aiby for a while. When I passed nearby, I overheard Aiby say, "They've all disappeared? And no one has found them? That's very interesting, Mr. Tiago."

I was curious. I stopped and asked, "What's wrong?"

Aiby turned to me. She looked like she'd just stepped down from the silvery moon in the sky. She hesitated as she always did when she was asked to share one of her many secrets. Aiby introduced me to Mr. Tiago, then leaned in close to me and whispered, "I still have a lot of things to explain —"

But I didn't wait for her to finish. "I know," I whispered back. "All in due time."

I proudly lifted my half-empty glass of apple juice in a toast. "It was a pleasure to meet you, Mr. Tiago," I said. "And Aiby, you look positively radiant this evening."

After delivering that ridiculous line, I bowed and walked away like some corny hero from a bad movie.

I joined Doug and my parents. A short while later, we were heading back home together as I wheeled my bike alongside me.

The moon's silvery glow peeped in and out from

behind the clouds as we walked, occasionally bathing the entire scene in spectral light. As I walked together with my family, I felt at peace. I finally understood that what Aiby had said was true: no one can know everything.

I'd learned to love the mystery of it all.

ENCHANTED EMPORIUM

36 EGGSTONES HEAVEN   APPLECROSS, SCOTLAND

PIERDOMENICO BACCALARIO

I was born on March 6, 1974, in Acqui
Terme, a small and beautiful town
of Piedmont, Italy. I grew up with my
three dogs, my black bicycle, and Andrea,
a special girl who lived five miles uphill
from my house.

© Walter Menegazzi

During my boring high school
classes, I often pretended to take notes
while I actually wrote stories. Around that
time, I also met a group of friends who
were fans of role-playing games. Together,
we invented and explored dozens of
fantastic worlds. I was always a curious but
quiet explorer.

While attending law school, I won an award for my novel,
The Road Warrior. It was one of the most beautiful days of my
entire life. From that moment on, I wrote and published my
novels. After graduating, I worked in museums and regaled
visitors with interesting stories about all the dusty, old objects
housed within.

Soon after, I started traveling. I visited Celle Ligure, Pisa,
Rome, Verona, London, and many other places. I've always loved
seeing new places and discovering new cultures, even if I always
end up back where I started.

There is one particular place that I love to visit: in the Susa
Valley, there's a tree you can climb that will let you see the most
magnificent landscape on the entire planet. If you don't mind long
walks, I will gladly tell you how to get there . . . as long as you
promise to keep it a secret.

Pierdomenico Baccalario

IACOPO BRUNO

I once had a very special friend who had everything he could possibly want. You see, ever since we were kids, he owned a magical pencil with two perfectly sharp ends. Whenever my friend wanted something, he drew it — and it came to life!

Once, he drew a spaceship — and we boarded it and went on a nice little tour around the galaxy.

Another time, he drew a sparkling red plane that was very similar to the Red Baron's, only a little smaller. He piloted us inside a giant volcano that had erupted only an hour earlier.

Whenever my friend was tired, he drew a big bed. We dreamed through the night until the morning light shone through the drawn shades.

This great friend of mine eventually moved to China . . . but he left his magic pencil with me!